Heathers The Musical

Book, Music & Lyrics by
Kevin Murphy & Laurence O'Keefe

Based on the film written by
Daniel Waters

Originally directed Off-Broadway by
Andy Fickman

Originally choreographed by
Marguerite Derricks

‖SAMUEL FRENCH‖

FOR PRODUCTION INQUIRIES

UNITED STATES AND CANADA
info@concordtheatricals.com
1-866-979-0447

UNITED KINGDOM AND EUROPE
licensing@concordtheatricals.co.uk
020-7054-7200

Each title is subject to availability from Concord Theatricals Corp., depending upon country of performance. Please be aware that *HEATHERS THE MUSICAL* may not be licensed by Concord Theatricals Corp. in your territory. Professional and amateur producers should contact the nearest Concord Theatricals Corp. office or licensing partner to verify availability.

The world premiere of *HEATHERS THE MUSICAL* opened Off-Broadway on March 31, 2014 at New World Stages. It was presented by Andy Cohen, Andy Fickman, J. Todd Harris, Kevin Murphy, Laurence O'Keefe, Amy Powers, Jamie Bendell, Bruce Bendell, Scott Benson, Scott Prisand in association with Big Block Entertainment, Bernard Abrams & Michael Speyer/StageVentures, Katie Leary/Vineyard Point Productions, Bill Prady, Karen J. Lauder, the Hasty Pudding Institute, Evan Todd, RJ Hendricks, and HIPZEE. The executive producer was Denise DiNovi in association with Lakeshore Entertainment.

This original production was directed by Andy Fickman, with choreography by Marguerite Derricks, fight direction by Rick Sordelet and Christian Kelly-Sordelet, sets by Timothy R. Mackabee, costumes by Amy Clark, lighting by Jason Lyons, hair/wigs/makeup by Leah Loukas, sound by Jonny Massena, musical direction by Dominick Amendum, and casting by Sheila Guthrie and Suzanne Goddard-Smythe. The production stage manager was Ritchard Druther, assisted by Cassie Apthorpe. Musical arrangements and orchestrations were by Laurence O'Keefe and Ben Green. Madeline Myers and Madeline Smith were music and score preparation assistants. Press representation was provided by Vivacity Media Group, with advertising/marketing by AKA and management by Roy Gabay Productions, Juniper Street Productions, Daniel Kuney, Mandy Tate, and Deirdre Murphy. The cast was as follows:

VERONICA SAWYER	Barrett Wilbert Weed
JASON "J.D." DEAN	Ryan McCartan
HEATHER CHANDLER	Jessica Keenan Wynn
HEATHER MCNAMARA	Elle McLemore
HEATHER DUKE	Alice Lee
MARTHA DUNNSTOCK	Katie Ladner
RAM SWEENEY	Jon Eidson
KURT KELLY	Evan Todd
RAM'S DAD / BIG BUD DEAN / COACH RIPPER	Anthony Crivello
MS. FLEMING / VERONICA'S MOM	Michelle Duffy
KURT'S DAD / VERONICA'S DAD / PRINCIPAL GOWAN	Daniel Cooney
BELEAGUERED GEEK	Dustin Sullivan
PREPPY STUD / OFFICER MILNER	AJ Meijer
HIPSTER DORK / OFFICER MCCORD	Dan Domenech
STONER CHICK	Rachel Flynn
YOUNG REPUBLICANETTE	Cait Fairbanks
NEW WAVE PARTY GIRL / DANCE CAPTAIN	Charissa Hogeland
SWINGS	Molly Hager, Matthew Schatz

The band was as follows:

Conductor / Keyboard . . . . Dominick Amendum
Guitars . . . . Austin Moorhead
Bass . . . . Steve Gilewski
Drums . . . . Greg Joseph
Trumpet / Flugelhorn . . . . John Dent
Reeds . . . . Steve Lyon
Violin . . . . Victoria Paterson
Synthesizer Consultant . . . . Randy Cohen
Synthesizer Programming . . . . Taylor Williams

The UK premiere of *HEATHERS THE MUSICAL* opened in London on June 19, 2018 at The Other Palace and subsequently transferred to Theatre Royal Haymarket, where it opened on September 3, 2018. It was presented by Bill Kenwright, Andrew Lloyd Webber, and Paul Taylor-Mills.

This production was directed by Andy Fickman, with choreography by Gary Lloyd, fight direction by Lisa Connell, music direction by Simon Budd, set and costume design by David Shields, lighting by Ben Cracknell, sound by Dan Samson, and casting by Will Burton. The production team included company stage managers Mark Wilkinson* and Helen Spall**, deputy stage managers Izzy Circou* and Ellie Muscutt**, stage manager/prop supervisor Natalia Sharville, asst. stage manager James Darnton, associate lighting designer/programmer Sarah Brown, assistant lighting designer Charlotte Burton, costume supervisor Pippa Batt, wardrobe head Rose Claridge, sound mixer #1 Isobel Rush, sound mixers #2 Ari Levy* and Dave Rymer**, lighting head James Horsington, and follow spot operators Ben Wilton, James Thorne** and James Rogers*. Musical arrangements and orchestrations were by Laurence O'Keefe and Ben Green, and music supervision was by Gary Hickeson and Rich Morris. Press representation was provided by Emma Holland PR, marketing by Dewynters, and social media consultation by Deirdre Murphy. The cast was as follows:

VERONICA SAWYER	Carrie Hope Fletcher
JASON "J.D." DEAN	Jamie Muscato
HEATHER CHANDLER	Jodie Steele
HEATHER MCNAMARA	Sophie Isaacs
HEATHER DUKE	T'Shan Williams
MARTHA DUNNSTOCK	Jenny O'Leary
RAM SWEENEY	Dominic Andersen
KURT KELLY	Christopher Chung
RAM'S DAD / BIG BUD DEAN / COACH RIPPER	Nathan Amzi*, Edward Baruwa**, Sergio Pasquariello***
MS. FLEMING / VERONICA'S MOM	Rebecca Lock
KURT'S DAD / VERONICA'S DAD / PRINCIPAL GOWAN	Jon Boydon
BELEAGUERED GEEK / OFFICER MILNER / ENSEMBLE	Alex James-Hatton
STONER CHICK / ENSEMBLE	Charlotte Jaconelli
NEW WAVE PARTY GIRL / ENSEMBLE	Lauren Drew
PREPPY STUD / OFFICER MCCORD / ENSEMBLE	Sergio Pasquariello***, Brandon Lee Sears*

YOUNG REPUBLICANETTE / ENSEMBLE . . . . Olivia Moore

HIPSTER DORK / ENSEMBLE . . . . John Lumsden*

DRAMA CLUB DRAMA QUEEN / ENSEMBLE . . . . .Merryl Ansah*

The band was as follows:

Conductor / Keyboard . . . . Simona Budd

Guitars . . . . Emily Linden

Bass . . . . Robyn Brown

Drums . . . . Becky Brass

Trumpet . . . . Georgina Bromilow*,

Rosanne Duckworth**

Reeds . . . . Katie Punter

*Royal Haymarket Production only
**The Other Palace Production only
***Sergio Pasquariello was ensemble track at The Other Palace and Haymarket. The actor cast as Ripper/Big Bud/Ram's Dad left the Haymarket production during previews and Sergio stepped in to open the show, eventually ceding the role to regular replacement Nathan Amzi. Sergio later left the show and was replaced by Brandon Lee Smith.

CHARACTERS

VERONICA SAWYER – (17) Burns to be both cool and kind, but doesn't yet know how to be both at the same time. Fierce sense of right and wrong, keen sense of ironic humor. Thinks she's an old soul, but she's still innocent enough to be blindsided by love or shocked by cruelty. Voice: high belting required, up to A♭. Must have dynamic and stylistic range.

JASON "J.D." DEAN – (17) Darkly charismatic, compelling, attractive. Charming on the outside, damaged on the inside. Keen smarts, savage wit. Voice: strong, confident belt to at least an A♭, A preferable; wide emotional range.

HEATHER CHANDLER – (17) The richest, hottest, cruelest girl in town. Relishes power and wields it without fear, patience, or mercy. Voice: strong belt to F or higher preferred. Mezzo for chorus. *NOTE: In certain choral songs,* **CHANDLER** *can switch parts with the other* **HEATHERS** *as needed.*

HEATHER MCNAMARA – (17) A beautiful cheerleader. Can be mean on command if Heather Chandler orders it, but actually quite vulnerable and fearful. Voice: strong belt to D♭, D preferred. Soprano for chorus. *NOTE: In certain choral songs,* **MCNAMARA** *and* **DUKE** *can switch vocal parts as needed.*

HEATHER DUKE – (17) The whipped beta dog of the three Heathers. Deeply insecure. When she finally becomes Queen Bee, she wields power like a bulldozer. Voice: strong belt to C, D preferred. Alto for chorus. *NOTE: In certain choral songs,* **DUKE** *and* **MCNAMARA** *can switch vocal parts as needed.*

MARTHA DUNNSTOCK – (17) Nicknamed "Martha Dumptruck," the opposite of confident and popular. Huge and beautiful soul, optimistic even in the face of rejection. Voice: strong belt to E or F, wide vocal expression.

RAM SWEENEY – (17) Linebacker. Big, insensitive to the feelings of others, ruled by appetites. Voice: strong baritone, belt to G, some falsetto useful. *NOTE: In certain songs,* **RAM** *and* **KURT** *can switch choral assignments if, say,* **RAM** *sings higher than* **KURT.**

KURT KELLY – (17) Quarterback and captain. Chiseled, rude, entitled, cocky. He's the brains in the friendship with Ram. Voice: tenor, strong belt to A♭ or A, some falsetto. *NOTE: In certain songs,* **KURT** *and* **RAM** *can switch choral assignments if, say,* **RAM** *sings higher than* **KURT.**

RAM'S DAD / BIG BUD DEAN / COACH RIPPER – (40-45)

> **RAM'S DAD:** Former football player turned suburban dad, has never outgrown his high school glory days. Hates weakness, but capable of soul-searching when tragedy strikes.

BIG BUD DEAN: J.D.'s single dad. Big jolly personality that barely conceals the enormous rage bubbling just below the surface. Quite possibly a serial bomber.

COACH RIPPER: Stalwart, man's man; quick to defend his players.

Voice: baritone/tenor, power Country/Gospel belt to A♭, higher welcome. *NOTE: Sometimes this actor has played* **PRINCIPAL GOWAN** *instead of* **BIG BUD / COACH**.

MS. FLEMING / VERONICA'S MOM – (45-50)

MS. FLEMING: Aging hippie teacher, still yearning for the day the Age of Aquarius reaches Ohio. Resentful of today's entitled youth, protective of the underdogs. Despite a penchant for self-promotion, genuinely cares about the students in her charge.

VERONICA'S MOM: Easygoing, yet capable of laying down the law.

Voice: great belt up to C, higher always welcome.

KURT'S DAD / VERONICA'S DAD / PRINCIPAL GOWAN – (30-45)

KURT'S DAD: Straight-laced, very conservative, also former football player. A simple guy, not book smart, you'd be happy to share a beer with him.

VERONICA'S DAD: Easygoing and distant.

PRINCIPAL GOWAN: Rumpled, burned out, hates conflict.

Voice: strong baritone/tenor, power Country/Gospel belt to G, even higher better. *NOTE: Sometimes this actor has played* **BIG BUD/COACH** *instead of* **PRINCIPAL GOWAN**.

BOY 1: BELEAGUERED GEEK – (16-18) An embittered social outcast. Voice: baritone (up to F#) or tenor (up to A).

BOY 2: PREPPY STUD – (16-18) Straightlaced, ambitious, blow-dried. Dreams of being even richer than his parents. Voice: bass (up to E) or baritone (up to G#).

BOY 3: HIPSTER DORK – (16-18) Thinks he's Ducky from *Pretty in Pink*. Voice: baritone (up to F#) or tenor (up to A).

GIRL 1: NEW WAVE GIRL – (16-18) She wants her MTV and dresses accordingly. Voice: belt to at least C# (a soprano up to high A/B is also a plus).

GIRL 2: STONER CHICK – (16-18) Smokes outside with the freaks in between classes. Her future's so bright she's gotta wear shades to hide her bloodshot eyes. Voice: belt to at least C# (a soprano up to high A/B is also a plus).

GIRL 3: YOUNG REPUBLICANETTE – (16-18) A tennis-playing, perky Student Council type. Voice: belt to at least C# (soprano up to high A/B is also a plus).

SETTING

Sherwood, a small suburban town in Ohio

TIME

1989

ACT ONE

Scene One

Scene Two

Scene Three

Scene Four

Scene Five

Scene Six

Scene Seven

Scene Eight

Scene Nine

Scene Ten

ACT TWO

PREFACE FROM THE AUTHORS

Like the song says: *This ain't no high school, this is the Thunderdome.* For many people, including the authors of this musical, high school is a bruising and confusing experience. Between the ages of fourteen and eighteen our bodies are doing peculiar things – we begin to look and feel very different at an alarming pace. Everything we learned about peer interaction growing up is now pretty much out the window. And just as we've begun to grow apart from our strongest supporters – our parents – we're consigned to the pressure cooker of high school with minimal adult supervision and every incentive to eat or be eaten. Some lucky students perch comfortably at the top of the food chain. But many more of us feel isolated, abandoned, or even hunted. For folks like us, the 1989 movie *Heathers* is the perfect distillation of that experience. It's savagely, blisteringly funny and uncomfortably truthful. We love this movie because many years ago, when we needed it, it reassured us that our experiences were not unique. We all feel like outsiders and weirdos. Everyone is clueless and scared. And that's OK.

Viewed today, the film *Heathers* resonates in new ways that were unthinkable when it first came out in the late eighties. In 2018, rage-fueled mass shootings have become commonplace. Bullying is now amplified and broadcast by the enormous power of social media. Aided by technology, cruelty becomes anonymous and pervasive. No longer stopping when school ends, it follows kids home into their bedrooms, computers, and phones. Cultural echo chambers have all but eradicated courtesy and empathy in public discourse. TV news and Twitter make their money by stoking rage in Us about the behavior of Them and vice versa.

This brings us to why we chose to adapt *Heathers* for the musical stage. We wanted to dive cannonball-style into questions like, "Why do people say and do such awful things to one another?" and, "How can we change? How can we do better?" We wanted to give our audience a chance to look at the most terrible aspects of human nature, laugh at them, and maybe find inspiration to combat these things with love instead of anger. And for people who dwell on the fringes, as we once did, we want to make it very clear: we are all in this together. You may feel adrift and frightened, but you are not alone. This lifeboat is crowded, but we can all help keep it afloat.

A WORD TO DIRECTORS

We originally designed *Heathers* to be a show that can be mounted just about anywhere. It works with a simple unit set and simple lights. Westerberg High can be suggested by little more than the sound of a school bell.

We kept our production values simple because we had a tight budget and wanted to save money to pay for seven musicians and nineteen singers making a big glorious noise. *Heathers* is an emotional show with a big, beating teenage heart – the characters experience feelings so deep and wide they can only be expressed in song: Love, life, and death. Despair, forgiveness, and reconciliation. These primal themes require musical expression on a large scale. If your production budget can support cool stuff like projections or realistic lockers or an actual muddy cow pasture onstage, by all means have at it. But we strongly suggest you protect your sound at all costs – we have found a good sound designer and equipment a better investment than super-intricate lighting or set designs. Support the score and your production will succeed.

The other big priority for us was the costumes. For the original production, that's what set the time, place, and tone. The three Heathers and Veronica were color-coordinated and fabulous. The students and faculty were costumed simply, but strongly evoked the eighties. *Heathers* audiences want their MTV. We suggest you give it to them.

Finally, a word about sincerity (lots, please!) and camp (less, please). We think this material is best served by honest emotion and life-and-death stakes. These characters don't know they're funny, so your actors should never mug or comment upon the extremity (or even absurdity) of the plot events. There are great online videos of brilliant drag queens lip-syncing wonderfully to some of *Heathers*' meaner songs. Their mile-a-minute bump-'n'-grind makes for a hilarious cabaret act. But the full show requires recognizable human beings, lunging for safety and happiness and love like a drowning man lunging for a lifeboat. Their realistic and relatable hopes, fears, pressures, and crises drive them to extraordinary actions.

So avoid adding ad-libs, inflating performances to cartoon size, or inserting extra lines or references from the (admittedly brilliant) movie. We will applaud when you focus on these characters trying to make positive fixes in their lives.

Yes, positive. Most villains don't think they're villains; they rationalize villainous behavior with, "It's what I had to do to fix my problem." So it is with *Heathers*. You'll get best results when your characters avoid excessive or gratuitous cruelty and negativity and instead play up solutions and hope. And solutions and hope, by stunning coincidence, are what we found in *Heathers*, and what we hope your audience will too.

Thank you gently with a chainsaw,
Kevin Murphy & Laurence O'Keefe

SPECIAL THANKS

The authors would like to thank each and every one of the producers, investors, cast, band, crew, and designers of our LA and NY productions and developmental readings, especially our partners Todd Harris, Andy Cohen, Amy Powers, Scott Prisand, Bruce Bendell and Jamie Bendell; also Tom Rosenberg, Gary Lucchesi, and Lakeshore as well as Michael Lehmann, Denise DiNovi, and un-Heather Dan Waters.

We owe a huge debt to John Buzzetti, Paul Haas, Lindsay Dunn, Nick Holly, Conrad Rippy, Barry Tyerman, Jamie Mandelbaum, Samuel French, Ritchard Druther, Betsy Sullenger, Marykate Meath, Erika McCormack, Kristen Gura Fickman, Nick Mueller, Michelle "Pinkie" Pinkney, Deirdre Murphy, and Michael Croiter, who did so much to help us build the show after our New York run.

We'd also like to acknowledge our talented friends in the UK who helped us workshop and further refine the show for the West End, especially Bill Kenwright, Andrew Lloyd Webber, Paul Taylor-Mills, Lily Caisley, Milly Summer, Lee Batty, Steve Potts, Tom DeKeyser, and Hamish Greer.

And a special shout-out to Sherwood's little Eskimo, Andy Fickman. You are the flag we pledge allegiance to.

To Nell & Persephone, Noreen & Carter – you make things beautiful.

ACT ONE

Scene One

(In darkness, a school bell rings.)

VERONICA. *(In darkness.)* September 1, 1989. Dear Diary:

[MUSIC NO. 01 "BEAUTIFUL (PART ONE)"]

(Lights up. Lunchtime at Westerberg High School. A school corridor opens into an outdoor lunch area with tables and chairs. Here and elsewhere, locations are represented loosely with lighting changes and/ or projections, as well as the minimal addition and subtraction of set pieces. Meet **VERONICA SAWYER,** *seventeen, smart and artsy.)*

I think I'm a good person. I believe there's good in everyone. But here we are, first day of senior year.

*(***STUDENTS*** mill about, members of various social cliques. Also present are some* **FACULTY MEMBERS:** *Jaded* **PRINCIPAL GOWAN,** *gruff jock* **COACH RIPPER,** *and eccentrically dressed ex-hippie teacher* **MS. FLEMING.**)*

I see these kids I've known all my life and wonder: What happened?

STUDENTS & FACULTY.
> FREAK! SLUT!
> BURNOUT! BUG-EYES!
> POSER! LARD-ASS!

VERONICA.
> WE WERE SO TINY.
> HAPPY AND SHINY.
> PLAYING TAG AND GETTING CHASED.

STUDENTS & FACULTY.
> FREAK! SLUT!
> LOSER! SHORT BUS!

VERONICA.
> SINGING AND CLAPPING,
> LAUGHING AND NAPPING.
> BAKING COOKIES, EATING PASTE.

STUDENTS & FACULTY.
> BULL-DYKE! STUCK-UP!
> HUNCHBACK!

VERONICA.
> THEN WE GOT BIGGER.
> THAT WAS THE TRIGGER
> LIKE THE HUNS INVADING ROME –

> *(Some* **STUDENTS** *push past* **VERONICA,** *nearly knocking her over.)*

STONER CHICK. Move.

> *(***VERONICA***'s not at fault, but apologizes anyway.)*

VERONICA. Sorry.
> WELCOME TO MY SCHOOL.
> THIS AIN'T NO HIGH SCHOOL;
> THIS IS THE THUNDERDOME.
> HOLD YOUR BREATH AND COUNT THE DAYS –
> WE'RE GRADUATING SOON.

STUDENTS & FACULTY.
> WHITE TRASH!

VERONICA.
> COLLEGE WILL BE PARADISE
> IF I'M NOT DEAD BY JUNE!

> *(Time shifts around her. The rest of the cast moves in slow motion.)*

> BUT I KNOW, I KNOW,
> LIFE CAN BE BEAUTIFUL.
> I PRAY, I PRAY
> FOR A BETTER WAY.
> IF WE CHANGED BACK THEN,

WE COULD CHANGE AGAIN.
WE CAN BE BEAUTIFUL...

*(Normal motion resumes. A **PREPPY STUD** shoves a* **HIPSTER DORK** *wearing a tragically un-hip fedora. The* **HIPSTER** *stumbles and falls.)*

HIPSTER. Ow!

VERONICA.

...JUST NOT TODAY.

*(She tries to help up the **HIPSTER**.)*

You okay?

HIPSTER. Get away, nerd!

*(**VERONICA** watches the **STUDENTS** line up for lunch.)*

STUDENTS & FACULTY.

FREAK! SLUT! CRIPPLE!
HOMO! HOMO! HOMO!

VERONICA.

THINGS WILL GET BETTER
SOON AS MY LETTER
COMES FROM HARVARD, DUKE, OR BROWN.
WAKE FROM THIS COMA,
TAKE MY DIPLOMA,
THEN I CAN BLOW THIS TOWN.
DREAM OF IVY-COVERED WALLS
AND SMOKY FRENCH CAFÉS...

*(**RAM SWEENEY**, a bulky linebacker, enters and walks up to the **PREPPY STUD**.)*

RAM. *(To **PREPPY**.)* Watch this...

VERONICA.

FIGHT THE URGE TO STRIKE A MATCH
AND SET THIS DUMP ABLAZE!

*(**RAM** upends **VERONICA**'s lunch tray.)*

RAM. Ooooops.

*(**EVERYONE** but **VERONICA** freezes.)*

VERONICA. *(To audience.)* Ram Sweeney. Third year as linebacker. And eighth year of smacking lunch trays and being a huge dick.

(Normal motion resumes.)

RAM. *(Heard her last two words.)* What did you say to me, skank?

VERONICA. …Nothing.

*(**RAM** gives **VERONICA** an "I got my eye on you" hand gesture and struts off past a **YOUNG REPUBLICANETTE** and **STONER CHICK**.)*

VERONICA.	**HIPSTER, PREPPY & RAM.**	**REPUBLICANETTE & STONER.**
BUT I KNOW,	I KNOW,	
I KNOW…	I KNOW…	I KNOW…
LIFE CAN BE		
BEAUTIFUL.	BEAUTIFUL.	BEAUTIFUL.
I PRAY…	I PRAY…	
I PRAY…	I PRAY…	I PRAY…
FOR A BETTER WAY.	FOR A BETTER WAY.	FOR A BETTER WAY.
WE WERE KIND BEFORE,	OO…	OO…
WE CAN BE KIND ONCE MORE;		
WE CAN BE BEAUTIFUL…	OO…	OO…
	BEAUTIFUL…	BEAUTIFUL…

*(**MARTHA DUNNSTOCK** enters. She's a senior, awkward, idiosyncratic dress and zero social currency. She comes up behind **VERONICA**, startling her.)*

VERONICA. Aaaagh!
    …HEY, MARTHA.
MARTHA. Hey.

*(**MARTHA** helps **VERONICA** pick up her lunch tray. **EVERYONE** but **VERONICA** freezes.)*

VERONICA. Martha Dunnstock. My best friend since diapers. She's got a huge heart. 'Round here, that's not enough.

(Normal motion resumes.)

Thanks.

MARTHA. We on for movie night?

VERONICA. You're on Jiffy Pop detail.

MARTHA. I rented *The Princess Bride.*

VERONICA. Again? Don't you have it memorized by now?

MARTHA. What can I say? I'm a sucker for a happy ending.

KURT. Martha Dumptruck!

(KURT KELLY approaches. He's a quarterback cool guy. He plucks a sandwich from MARTHA's tray.)

If you want to slim down…

(He pokes his middle finger through the center of MARTHA's sandwich and holds it up, flipping her the bird.)

You need more protein in your diet.

(EVERYONE but VERONICA freezes.)

VERONICA. Kurt Kelly. Quarterback. He is the smartest guy on the football team. Which is kind of like being the tallest dwarf.

(Normal motion resumes. KURT drops the sandwich back onto MARTHA's tray.)

What is wrong with you?

KURT. I'm sorry, are you actually talking to me?

(RAM steps up, a loyal wingman.)

RAM. My buddy Kurt asked you a question.

(STUDENTS observe, grateful this isn't happening to them. VERONICA takes a deep breath and goes on the offensive, turning to KURT.)

VERONICA. What gives you the right to pick on my friend? Look at you, you're a high school has-been waiting to happen. A future gas station attendant.

(Tense beat. KURT *points to her chin.)*

KURT. You got a zit right there.

(The STUDENTS *laugh.* KURT *shoves* VERONICA, *who stumbles back.* MARTHA *catches her.* VERONICA *pulls away from* MARTHA, *humiliated and angry.)*

VERONICA.
Dear Diary…

	BELEAGUERED GEEK.
WHY…	WHY DO THEY HATE ME?
	YOUNG REPUBLICANETTE.
	WHY DON'T I FIGHT BACK?
	KURT.
	WHY DO I ACT LIKE SUCH A CREEP?
WHY…	NEW WAVE GIRL.
	WHY WON'T HE DATE ME?
	HIPSTER DORK. *(Holding his fedora,*
	newly disenchanted.)
	WHY DID I WEAR THIS?
	STONER, PREPPY & MS. FLEMING.
	WHY DO I CRY MYSELF TO SLEEP?
	STUDENTS & FACULTY.
WHY…	SOMEBODY HUG ME!
	SOMEBODY FIX ME!
	SOMEBODY SAVE ME!
SEND ME A SIGN, GOD!	SEND ME A SIGN, GOD!
GIVE ME SOME HOPE	GIVE ME SOME HOPE HERE!
HERE!	
SOMETHING TO LIVE	SOMETHING TO LIVE FOR!
FOR!	

[MUSIC NO. 01A "BEAUTIFUL (PART TWO)"]

(The STUDENTS *form an honor guard as the three* HEATHERS *enter in wedge formation, unhurried, confident, magic.)*

STUDENTS & FACULTY.
AH…HEATHER. HEATHER…AND HEATHER!

VERONICA. Then there's the Heathers. They float above it all.

STUDENTS & FACULTY.
I LOVE HEATHER, HEATHER…AND HEATHER!

(VERONICA indicates HEATHER MCNAMARA, peppy and pretty.)

VERONICA.

Heather McNamara. Head cheerleader. Her dad's loaded – he sells engagement rings.

STUDENTS & FACULTY.

I HATE HEATHER, HEATHER... AND HEATHER!

(VERONICA indicates HEATHER DUKE, whipped beta-dog of the trio, insecure and ambitious.)

Heather Duke. Runs the yearbook. No discernible personality, but her mom did pay for implants.

I WANT HEATHER, HEATHER... AND HEATHER!

(VERONICA indicates HEATHER CHANDLER, the ruthless, brutal queen bee.)

And Heather Chandler. The Almighty.

I NEED HEATHER, HEATHER...

VERONICA. She is a mythic bitch.

(Then:)

The Heathers are solid Teflon – never bothered, never harassed. I would give anything to be like that.

HIPSTER DORK.

I'd like to be their boyfriend.
THAT WOULD BE
    BEAUTIFUL...

STUDENTS & FACULTY.

MM...

THAT WOULD BE
    BEAUTIFUL...

STONER CHICK.

If I sat at their table, guys would notice me.

MM...
SO BEAUTIFUL...

MARTHA.

I'd like them to be nicer.
THAT WOULD BE
    BEAUTIFUL.

OO...
THAT WOULD BE
    BEAUTIFUL.

BELEAGUERED GEEK.	STUDENTS & FACULTY.
I'd like to kidnap a Heather and photograph her naked in an abandoned warehouse and leave her tied up for the rats!	OO...

(The bell rings. We're now in the girls' bathroom.)

*(**VERONICA** enters, quietly observing our three lovely predators in their natural habitat.)*

*(**CHANDLER** and **MCNAMARA** apply makeup in the mirror as **DUKE** vomits into a toilet.)*

CHANDLER. Grow up, Heather. Bulimia is so '87.

DUKE. *(Woozy.)* Heather, I need a mint.

*(**MCNAMARA** extracts a roll of breath mints from her purse and hands one to **DUKE**, who pops it into her mouth.)*

MCNAMARA. What you need, Heather, is to see a doctor.

*(**DUKE** is about to respond but hesitates, suddenly nauseous. She turns back to the toilet.)*

*(**MS. FLEMING** enters.)*

*(Ignored by **MS. FLEMING**, **VERONICA** scribbles on a piece of paper.)*

MS. FLEMING. Ah, Heather and Heather.

*(**DUKE** vomits.)*

And Heather. Perhaps you didn't hear the bell over all the vomiting. You're late for class.

CHANDLER. Heather wasn't feeling well. We're helping her.

MS. FLEMING. Not without a hall pass you're not. A week's detention.

*(Three **HEATHERS** overlapping:)*

DUKE. What? No way, that's not fair. .

MCNAMARA. But I've got cheerleader practice.

CHANDLER. My parents pay your salary!

VERONICA. Actually, Ms. Fleming…

(She hands FLEMING a pass.)

…all four of us are out *on* a hall pass. Yearbook committee.

(MS. FLEMING sourly examines the pass as the HEATHERS exchange puzzled looks.)

MS. FLEMING. I see you're all listed. Hurry up and get where you're going.

(She exits. CHANDLER grabs the pass from VERONICA and studies it.)

CHANDLER. This is an excellent forgery. Who are you?

(VERONICA cheerfully extends her hand. CHANDLER ignores the gesture.)

VERONICA. Veronica Sawyer. I crave a boon.

CHANDLER. What boon?

VERONICA. Let me sit at your table at lunch. Just once. No talking necessary. If people think you guys tolerate me, they'll leave me alone. Before you answer, I also do report cards, permission slips, and absence notes.

(CHANDLER smiles, tickled by VERONICA's boldness. DUKE sneers with contempt.)

DUKE. How about prescriptions?

CHANDLER. Shut up, Heather.

DUKE. Sorry, Heather.

(CHANDLER brushes back VERONICA's hair and inspects her face.)

CHANDLER. Hmm. For a greasy little nobody, you do have good bone structure.

MCNAMARA. And a symmetrical face. If I took a meat cleaver down the center of your skull, I'd have matching halves. That's very important.

DUKE. Of course, you could stand to lose a few pounds.

CHANDLER.

AND YA KNOW, YA KNOW, YA KNOW?

(Tipping **VERONICA***'s chin.)* THIS COULD BE BEAUTIFUL.

MASCARA, MAYBE SOME LIP GLOSS...

AND WE'RE ON OUR WAY.

GET THIS GIRL SOME BLUSH

AND HEATHER, I NEED YOUR BRUSH,

LET'S MAKE HER BEAUTIFUL...

DUKE.

LET'S MAKE HER BEAUTIFUL...

MCNAMARA.

LET'S MAKE HER BEAUTIFUL...

CHANDLER.

MAKE HER BEAUTIFUL...

Okay?

VERONICA. Okay!

(The **HEATHERS** *exit with* **VERONICA***.)*

(The school bell rings. Another day, another lunch.)

*(***KURT** *and* **RAM** *enter and push aside the* **BELEAGUERED GEEK***.)*

KURT.

OUT OF MY WAY, GEEK!

BELEAGUERED GEEK.

I DON'T WANT TROUBLE –

RAM.

YOU'RE GONNA DIE AT THREE P.M.!

(He shoves the **BELEAGUERED GEEK** *into the* **YOUNG REPUBLICANETTE** *and* **NEW WAVE GIRL***.)*

YOUNG REPUBLICANETTE & NEW WAVE GIRL.

DON'T YOU DARE TOUCH ME!

GET AWAY, PERVERT!

BELEAGUERED GEEK. *(Bewildered and scared.)*

WHAT'D I EVER DO TO THEM?

STUDENTS & FACULTY.

WHO COULD SURVIVE THIS?

I CAN'T ESCAPE THIS!

I THINK I'M DYING!

MS. FLEMING. *(Sees someone offstage.)*

WHO'S THAT WITH HEATHER?

ALL. Whoa!

*(The **HEATHERS** enter again, but this time there's someone with them…)*

STUDENTS & FACULTY.

HEATHER, HEATHER, HEATHER…

NEW WAVE GIRL.

AND…SOMEONE!

STUDENTS & FACULTY.

HEATHER, HEATHER, HEATHER…

STONER CHICK, PREPPY STUD & BELEAGUERED GEEK.

AND A BABE!

STUDENTS & FACULTY.

HEATHER, HEATHER, HEATHER…

MARTHA. *(Recognizing her.)*

VERONICA?

STUDENTS & FACULTY.

VERONICA? VERONICA! VERONICA!!

*(The **HEATHERS** part, revealing **VERONICA**, who's been given a makeover – she's smoking hot.)*

VERONICA.	**STUDENTS & FACULTY.**
AND YA KNOW,	OH!
YA KNOW, YA KNOW…	AH!
LIFE CAN BE BEAUTIFUL.	BEAUTIFUL!
YOU HOPE, YOU DREAM,	OH!
YOU PRAY,	AH!
AND YOU GET YOUR WAY!	BEAUTIFUL!
ASK ME HOW IT FEELS	
LOOKING LIKE	
HELL ON WHEELS…	OOH, OOH! AH!
MY GOD, IT'S BEAUTIFUL!	BEAUTIFUL!…
I MIGHT BE BEAUTIFUL!	BEAUTIFUL!…
AND WHEN YOU'RE	
BEAUTIFUL…	AH…

VERONICA.
IT'S A BEAUTIFUL FRICKIN'
DAY!

STUDENTS & FACULTY.
HEATHER! HEATHER!
HEATHER!
VERONICA!

HEY!

HEATHER! HEATHER!
HEATHER!
VERONICA! VERONICA!
VERONICA! VERONICA!
VERONICA!

VERONICA! VERONICA!
VERONICA!

(Song ends. Blackout.)

Scene Two

[MUSIC NO. 01B "IT'S BEEN THREE WEEKS"]

(School. Yet another lunchtime. **VERONICA** *writes in her diary.)*

VERONICA. Dear Diary: It's been three weeks since I became friends with the Heathers.

(She crosses something out.)

"Friends" isn't the right word, exactly. It's more like the Heathers are people I work with and our job is being popular and shit.

(The bell rings. **MARTHA** *enters. There's a whiff of tension between the two friends.)*

MARTHA. Hey, Veronica.

VERONICA. Hey.

MARTHA. You really look beautiful these days.

VERONICA. Yeah, well, it's still the same me underneath.

MARTHA. Are you sure?

VERONICA. Look, I'm sorry I flaked on movie night last week. I've had a lot going on.

MARTHA. I get that. You're with the Heathers now. It's exciting.

VERONICA. It's whatever. But we'll hang soon, I promise.

(DUKE enters.) Dourstage right

DUKE. Veronica! Heather requires your presence. Now.

VERONICA. How very.

(VERONICA and DUKE cross the schoolyard. They pass a figure leaning against the wall.)

(Meet **JASON DEAN,** *a.k.a. "J.D.," a moody suburban rebel. He's reading a copy of Baudelaire's* Flowers of Evil.*)*

(VERONICA and DUKE approach the Heathers' designated lunch table.)

(CHANDLER waits impatiently with MCNAMARA.)

CHANDLER. Veronica, I need a forgery in Ram Sweeney's handwriting. You'll need something to write on. Heather, bend over.

(**DUKE** *bends over to allow* **VERONICA** *to write on her back. It's degrading, but she's used to it.* **VERONICA** *writes as* **CHANDLER** *dictates.*)

"Hi, Beautiful – I've been watching you…and thinking about us in the old days. I hope you can come to my homecoming party this weekend. I miss you… Ram." Put an "XO" after the signature.

VERONICA. What's this for anyway?

CHANDLER. You remember how Ram used to hang with Martha Dumptruck?

VERONICA. Well yeah, in kindergarten. We all did.

DUKE. We *all* didn't kiss on the kickball field.

MCNAMARA. *(Suddenly excited.)* Oh my God, that's right! I totally forgot. Ram kissed Martha Dumptruck.
(Delighted glee.) It was disgusting!

CHANDLER. *(Takes the note.)* Perfect.

(**KURT** *and* **RAM** *enter.*)

Ram, c'mere!

RAM. Whaddaya think Heather wants?

KURT. My hot bod-aay!

RAM. Hell, yeah. Punch it in.

(**RAM** *and* **KURT** *"punch it in" by bumping fists. It's a thing with them.* **CHANDLER** *holds up the note.*)

CHANDLER. Be a sweetie and give this note to Martha Dumptruck for me.

VERONICA. What? No!

(*Before* **RAM** *can take it,* **VERONICA** *snatches it from* **CHANDLER**'s *hand.*)

VERONICA. Martha's had a crush on Ram for like twelve years now, this will kill her. C'mon, Heather, you're bigger than this.

[MUSIC NO. 02 "CANDY STORE"]

CHANDLER.

ARE WE GONNA HAVE A PROBLEM?
YOU GOT A BONE TO PICK?
YOU'VE COME SO FAR;
WHY NOW ARE YOU
PULLING ON MY DICK?
I'D NORMALLY SLAP YOUR FACE OFF,
AND EVERYONE HERE COULD WATCH.
BUT I'M FEELING NICE.
HERE'S SOME ADVICE.
LISTEN UP, BYATCH.

(The **HEATHERS** *advance on* **VERONICA**, *smiling in tight formation like Satan's favorite girl group. Three* **ENSEMBLE GIRLS** *sing along with the* **HEATHERS** *but should be removed from the action onstage.)*

CHANDLER.	**DUKE, MCNAMARA & GIRLS.**
I LIKE	I LIKE!
LOOKING HOT.	
BUYING STUFF THEY CAN NOT.	
I LIKE	I LIKE!
DRINKING HARD.	
MAXING DAD'S CREDIT CARD.	
I LIKE	I LIKE!
SKIPPING GYM.	
SCARING HER. SCREWING HIM.	
I LIKE	I LIKE!
KILLER CLOTHES.	

CHANDLER.	**DUKE, MCNAMARA & GIRLS.**
KICKING NERDS IN THE NOSE!	KICKING NERDS IN THE NOSE!

IF YOU LACK THE BALLS,
YOU CAN GO PLAY DOLLS;

CHANDLER.
LET YOUR MOMMY FIX YOU
 A SNACK.   **DUKE, MCNAMARA & GIRLS.**
                            WHOA, OH!

OR YOU COULD COME
 SMOKE,
POUND SOME RUM AND
 COKE,
IN MY PORSCHE WITH THE
 QUARTERBACK!

                            OH WHOA! OH WHOA! OH
                            WHOA!

CHANDLER, DUKE, MCNAMARA & GIRLS.
HONEY, WHAT YOU WAITING FOR?
WELCOME TO MY CANDY STORE!
TIME FOR YOU TO PROVE
YOU'RE NOT A LOSER ANYMORE...
THEN STEP INTO MY CANDY STORE!...

GUYS FALL

DUKE & MCNAMARA.
AT YOUR FEET.

DUKE.
PAY THE CHECK!

MCNAMARA.
HELP YOU CHEAT!

CHANDLER, DUKE, MCNAMARA & GIRLS.
ALL YOU

DUKE.
HAVE TO DO?

CHANDLER.
SAY GOODBYE TO SHAMU.

CHANDLER, DUKE, MCNAMARA & GIRLS.
THAT FREAK'S

MCNAMARA.
NOT YOUR FRIEND.
I CAN TELL, IN THE END,

CHANDLER, DUKE, MCNAMARA & GIRLS.

IF SHE

DUKE.

HAD YOUR SHOT,

CHANDLER, DUKE, MCNAMARA & GIRLS.

SHE WOULD LEAVE YOU TO ROT!

MCNAMARA.

'COURSE, IF YOU DON'T CARE,
FINE, GO BRAID HER HAIR.
MAYBE *SESAME STREET* IS ON.

CHANDLER, DUKE & GIRLS.

WHOA, WHOA!

(During this, CHANDLER retrieves VERONICA's note and passes it to DUKE.)

MCNAMARA.

OR FORGET THAT CREEP,

DUKE.

AND GET IN MY JEEP...

CHANDLER.

LET'S GO TEAR UP SOMEONE'S LAWN!

DUKE, MCNAMARA & GIRLS.

OH WHOA! OH WHOA! OH WHOA!

(As the HEATHERS pass MARTHA, DUKE slips the note onto her lunch tray.)

CHANDLER, DUKE, MCNAMARA & GIRLS.

HONEY, WHAT YOU WAITING FOR?
WELCOME TO MY CANDY STORE!
YOU JUST GOTTA PROVE YOU'RE NOT A PUSSY ANYMORE...
THEN STEP INTO MY CANDY STORE!

(MARTHA opens the note and reads it.)

CHANDLER.

YOU CAN JOIN THE TEAM...

DUKE, MCNAMARA & GIRLS.

OR YOU CAN BITCH AND MOAN.

CHANDLER.

YOU CAN LIVE THE DREAM...

DUKE, MCNAMARA & GIRLS.

OR YOU CAN DIE ALONE.

CHANDLER.

YOU CAN FLY WITH EAGLES,   **DUKE, MCNAMARA & GIRLS.**
OR IF YOU PREFER,   OR IF YOU PREFER,
KEEP ON TESTING ME
AND END UP LIKE HER!   AND END UP LIKE HER!

(MARTHA hurries up, waving the forged "note from Ram.")

MARTHA. Veronica, look! Ram invited me to his homecoming party! See? I told you there was still something there. This *proves* he's been thinking about me!

(VERONICA glances over at the HEATHERS. CHANDLER gives VERONICA a "Who's it going to be?" look.)

VERONICA. ...Color me stoked.

MARTHA. I'm so happy.

(She exits. Now it's DUKE's turn to solo – she wails, making the most of her moment...)

DUKE. *(Wailing vocal ad-lib.)*   **GIRLS.**
OH, OH, OH, OH, OH!   WHOA, WHOA!
HONEY, WHATCHA WAITIN'
     FOR!

(CHANDLER shoves DUKE out of the way.)

CHANDLER.

Shut up, Heather.
(Wailing vocal ad-lib.)
STEP INTO MY CANDAAAY   **DUKE, MCNAMARA & GIRLS.**
     STORE,   WHOA!
                             TIME FOR YOU TO PROVE
WHOA...!   YOU'RE NOT A LAME-ASS
                             ANYMORE...
                             THEN STEP INTO MY
                                  CANDY STORE!

HEATHERS & GIRLS.

IT'S MY CANDY STORE. IT'S MY CANDY...

IT'S MY CANDY STORE! IT'S MY CANDY...
IT'S MY CANDY STORE! IT'S MY CANDY STO...
...ORE!

(Song ends. The **HEATHERS** *flounce off.* **VERONICA** *starts to exit, passing* **J.D.** *He speaks to her without looking up from his book.)*

J.D. You shouldn't have bowed down to the Swatch-dogs and Diet-Cokeheads. They're gonna crush that girl.

VERONICA. I'm sorry, what?

J.D. You've clearly got a soul. You just need to work harder keeping it clean. We are all born marked for evil.

(He shuts his book and walks away.)

VERONICA. Okay, don't quote Baudelaire at me and walk away, excuse me? Didn't catch your name.

J.D. I didn't throw it.

(He continues moving off. **VERONICA** *smiles, intrigued despite herself.)*

*(***KURT** *and* **RAM** *have been watching* **J.D.**'s *exchange with* **VERONICA.**)*

KURT. Who does that guy in the jacket think he is anyways, Bo Diddley?

RAM. Veronica's into his act, no doubt.

KURT. Let's kick his ass.

RAM. We're seniors, man. Too old for this.

*(***KURT** *approaches* **J.D.** *anyway.* **RAM** *follows, reluctant but dutiful.)*

KURT. Hey, sweetheart. What did your boyfriend say when you told him you were moving to Sherwood, Ohio?

*(***RAM** *gets in* **J.D.**'s *face.)*

RAM. My buddy Kurt just asked you a question.

KURT. Hey Ram, doesn't this cafeteria have a "no fags allowed" rule?

*(***J.D.** *eyes him for a beat, then:)*

J.D. I don't know what your problem is, but I bet it's really hard for you to pronounce.

(**STUDENTS** *gasp. Nobody but nobody at this school talks smack to football gods – until now.* **KURT** *smiles at* **J.D.** *for a beat…then signals* **RAM**.)

KURT. Hold his arms!

[MUSIC NO. 03 "FIGHT FOR ME"]

(**KURT** *takes a swing at* **J.D.**, *who dodges and manages to slip loose from* **RAM**.)

(**J.D.** *blocks a punch from* **RAM** *with his Baudelaire book. He then cracks* **RAM** *across the face with it, then* **KURT**.)

GIRLS.

HOLY SHIT!

GUYS.

HOLY SHIT!

GIRLS.

HOLY SHIT!

GUYS.

HOLY SHIT!

GIRLS.

HOLY SHIT!

ALL.

HOLY SHIT!

HOLY SHIT!

HOLY SHIT!

HOLY SHIT!

(*As* **J.D.** *pulls back his fist, positioned to punch* **KURT** *in the face, the fight freezes. Time has stopped for everyone except* **VERONICA**.)

VERONICA.

WHY, WHEN YOU SEE BOYS FIGHT,

DOES IT LOOK SO HORRIBLE, YET…

FEEL SO RIGHT?

I SHOULDN'T WATCH THIS CRAP;

THAT'S NOT WHO I AM.

BUT WITH THIS KID...
DAAAAAMN.

*(She walks around the immobile **J.D.**, fascinated.)*

HEY,
MISTER NO-NAME KID,
SO WHO MIGHT YOU BE?
AND COULD YOU FIGHT FOR ME?
AND HEY,
COULD YOU FACE THE CROWD?
COULD YOU BE SEEN WITH ME
AND STILL ACT PROUD?

HEY,
WOULD YOU HOLD MY HAND?
AND COULD YOU CARRY ME
THROUGH NO MAN'S LAND?
IT'S FINE IF YOU DON'T AGREE,
BUT I WOULD FIGHT FOR YOU...
IF YOU WOULD FIGHT FOR ME.

(The fight resumes in slow motion.)

VERONICA.	**STUDENTS & FACULTY.**
LET THEM DRIVE US UNDERGROUND.	AHHHH... AHHHH...
I DON'T CARE HOW FAR.	AHHHH...
YOU CAN SET MY BROKEN BONES,	AHHHH...
AND I KNOW C.P.R.	AHHHH...

*(**VERONICA** examines **J.D.** as his fist makes slow-mo contact with **RAM**'s chin.)*

WELL, WHOA!

VERONICA.
YOU CAN PUNCH REAL
GOOD.
YOU'VE LASTED LONGER
THAN I THOUGHT YOU
WOULD.
SO HEY,
MISTER NO-NAME KID,

VERONICA.

IF SOME NIGHT YOU'RE FREE...	**STUDENTS & FACULTY.** AHHHH... AHHHH... AHHHH...

(The slow-motion fight continues. **J.D.** *kicks serious ass, headbutting* **RAM** *three times, then tossing him aside.)*

WANNA FIGHT FOR ME? IF YOU'RE STILL ALIVE... I WOULD FIGHT FOR YOU... IF YOU WOULD FIGHT FOR ME...	HOLY SHIT... HOLY SHIT... HOLY SHIT, HOLY SHIT, HOLY SHIT, HOLY SHIT, HOLY SHIT, HOLY SHIT.

(Song ends. The fight is over. **KURT** *and* **RAM** *are down.* **J.D.** *wins! Blackout.)*

(The following optional cue may be used over the scene change if required.)

[MUSIC NO. 03A "TRANSITION TO CROQUET"]

*(***J.D.*** *exits as* **KURT** *and* **RAM** *pick themselves up off the ground.)*

KURT. Man, that sucked.

RAM. Those were some cheap shots.

KURT. Ow! I'm missing a ball!

RAM. No, you're not.

KURT. Seriously, I think he knocked it up my butt or something.

RAM. It's probably impacted. Plug your nose and push.

*(***KURT*** *holds his nose and grunts.)*

KURT. Okay, there it is.

*(***RAM*** *and* **KURT** *touch fists and exit. Lights change to...)*

Scene Three

(Veronica's backyard. Simple suburban, perhaps the lower end of the middle-class spectrum. There's a little garden table where Veronica's MOM and DAD sit. MOM applies spread to a snack cracker. DAD reads a spy novel.)

(The HEATHERS and VERONICA are finishing up a game of croquet.)

CHANDLER. *(Teasing.)* Your mouth was hanging open.

VERONICA. *(Laughs.)* No it wasn't.

CHANDLER. I mean, seriously, Veronica – drool much?

VERONICA. It was nothing like that.

CHANDLER. Come on, admit it, you like the new kid.

VERONICA. I don't even know his name.

DUKE. You were totally throwing your panties at him –

CHANDLER. *(Interrupting DUKE, annoyed.)* – Talking to my friend!

DUKE. Sorry, Heather.

(CHANDLER hits a ball out of play in the direction of MOM and DAD.)

VERONICA. Mom, Dad! Look out!

(MOM picks up the ball. CHANDLER crosses to retrieve it.)

MOM. Here you go, girls. Care for some pâté?

(CHANDLER inspects the plate, suspicious.)

CHANDLER. This isn't pâté. It's liverwurst.

MOM. *(Concealing irritation.)* I'm aware of that, Heather. It's a family joke.

CHANDLER. Oh. Funny.

(VERONICA hurries over for damage control.)

(DAD looks up from his book, apparently speaking to nobody in particular.)

DAD. Doggone it, will somebody please tell me why I read these spy novels?

VERONICA. 'Cause you're an idiot, Dad.

DAD. Oh yeah, that's it.

MOM. You two.

(**VERONICA** *squirms, acutely aware of* **CHANDLER**'s *judgmental smirk.*)

So girls. Any plans for tonight?

VERONICA. Big homecoming party at Ram Sweeney's house. I'm catching a ride with Heather.

(**CHANDLER** *taps her Swatch.*)

CHANDLER. Speaking of which…

VERONICA. Right. Great pâté, Mom, but we have to motor if we want to be ready for that party.

(**CHANDLER** *plops the croquet ball into the "pâté"…*)

CHANDLER. Oops.

MOM. Clean that. Right now.

CHANDLER. Do I look like the maid? Veronica, your mom is hilarious.

(*She exits. The other two* **HEATHERS** *follow her out.*)

(**VERONICA** *starts to follow, but* **MOM** *takes her arm.*)

MOM. I forbid you to go anywhere with that girl.

VERONICA. Mom.

MOM. She has no respect for anything.

VERONICA. I know what she is. What they all are. But they will get me safely through high school. I'm not gonna change, I promise.

(*Beat.*)

Can I go?

(**MOM** *considers, sighs, and nods "Go on, get out of here."*)

VERONICA. Thanks.

(*She kisses* **MOM** *on the cheek and exits.*)

MOM. What the hell goes on at that school?

DAD. *(Laughs, shaking head.)* I do *not* want to know.

(Lights out on **MOM** *and* **DAD**.*)*

(The following optional cue may be used over the scene change if required.)

[MUSIC NO. 03B "CANDY STORE PLAYOFF"]

HEATHERS & GIRLS.

SO STEP INTO MY CANDY STORE!
IT'S MY CANDY STORE. IT'S MY CANDY...
IT'S MY CANDY STORE, IT'S MY CANDY...
IT'S MY CANDY STORE, IT'S MY CANDY STORE!
...ORE!

Scene Four

(A 7-Eleven convenience store counter with candy, snacks, frozen-drink dispenser. **VERONICA** *enters.)*

(We hear a car horn from outside.)

CHANDLER. *(Offstage.)* Veronica! Don't forget to buy Corn Nuts! It's not a party without Corn Nuts!

*(***VERONICA*** *yells back over her shoulder:)*

VERONICA. Yes, Heather! Plain or BQ?

CHANDLER. *(Offstage.)* BQ!!

*(***VERONICA*** *picks out a bag of Corn Nuts.* **J.D.** *walks up.)*

J.D. Greetings and salutations. You want a Slurpee with that?

VERONICA. No, but if you're nice I'll let you buy me a Big Gulp.

J.D. That's like going to Mickey D's to order a salad. Slurpee's the signature dish of the house. Did you say cherry or lime?

VERONICA. I said Big Gulp. I'm Veronica, by the way. Veronica Sawyer. You ever gonna tell me your name?

J.D. I'll end the suspense. Jason Dean. J.D. for short.

VERONICA. So, "J.D." That thing you pulled in the caf was pretty severe.

J.D. The extreme always seems to make an impression.

VERONICA. What brings a Baudelaire-quoting bad-ass like you to Sherwood, Ohio?

J.D. My dad's work. He owns a de-construction company.

VERONICA. "De-construction"?

J.D. The old man seems to enjoy tearing things down. Seen the commercial? "I'm Big Bud Dean. If it's in the way, I'll make your day…"

VERONICA. Right, then he pushes the plunger and the screen blows up. That's your dad?

J.D. In all his toxic glory.

VERONICA. Well, everyone's life has got static.

(We hear the car horn again, this time more insistent.)

CHANDLER. *(Offstage.)* Veronica!!

VERONICA. Example. I don't really like my friends.

J.D. I don't like your friends either. Bag the party. Hang here.

[MUSIC NO. 04 "FREEZE YOUR BRAIN"]

VERONICA. At the 7-Eleven? Swanky first date.

J.D. Hey, I love this place.

VERONICA. No offense, but why?

J.D.

I'VE BEEN THROUGH TEN HIGH SCHOOLS.
THEY START TO GET BLURRY.
NO POINT PLANTING ROOTS,
'CAUSE YOU'RE GONE IN A HURRY.
MY DAD KEEPS TWO SUITCASES PACKED IN THE DEN,
SO IT'S ONLY A MATTER OF WHEN.

I DON'T LEARN THE NAMES,
DON'T BOTHER WITH FACES.
ALL I CAN TRUST IS THIS CONCRETE OASIS.
SEEMS EVERY TIME I'M ABOUT TO DESPAIR,
THERE'S A 7-ELEVEN RIGHT THERE.

EACH STORE IS THE SAME,
FROM LAS VEGAS TO BOSTON,
LINOLEUM AISLES THAT I LOVE TO GET LOST IN.
I PRAY AT MY ALTAR OF SLUSH;
YEAH, I LIVE FOR THAT SWEET FROZEN RUSH –

(He takes a hit of his Slurpee. He grimaces from the "brain freeze.")

FREEZE YOUR BRAIN,
SUCK ON THAT STRAW,
GET LOST IN THE PAIN.
HAPPINESS COMES
WHEN EV'RYTHING NUMBS.

J.D.

    WHO NEEDS COCAINE?
    FREEZE YOUR BRAIN.
    FREEZE YOUR BRAIN...

    (He offers the Slurpee to **VERONICA.***)*

    Care for a hit?

VERONICA. Does your mommy know you eat all this crap?

J.D. Not anymore.

    *(***VERONICA** *winces. Reminding a hot guy of a dead parent is a first date no-no.)*

    WHEN MOM WAS ALIVE
    WE LIVED HALFWAY NORMAL.
    BUT NOW IT'S JUST ME AND MY DAD.
    WE'RE LESS FORMAL.
    I LEARNED TO COOK PASTA,
    I LEARNED TO PAY RENT.
    LEARNED THE WORLD DOESN'T OWE YOU A CENT.

    YOU'RE PLANNING YOUR FUTURE,
    VERONICA SAWYER.
    YOU'LL GO TO SOME COLLEGE,
    THEN MARRY A LAWYER.
    BUT THE SKY'S GONNA HURT WHEN IT FALLS,
    SO YOU'D BETTER START BUILDING SOME WALLS...

    FREEZE YOUR BRAIN.
    SWIM IN THE ICE,
    GET LOST IN THE PAIN.
    SHUT YOUR EYES TIGHT,
    TILL YOU VANISH FROM SIGHT,
    LET NOTHING REMAIN –

    FREEZE YOUR BRAIN,
    SHATTER YOUR SKULL,
    FIGHT PAIN WITH MORE PAIN.
    FORGET WHO YOU ARE,
    UNBURDEN YOUR LOAD,
    FORGET IN SIX WEEKS
    YOU'LL BE BACK ON THE ROAD.

WHEN THE VOICE IN YOUR HEAD
SAYS YOU'RE BETTER OFF DEAD,
DON'T OPEN A VEIN –
JUST FREEZE YOUR BRAIN.
FREEZE YOUR BRAIN.
GO ON AND FREEZE YOUR BRAIN...

Try it.

(Song ends. **VERONICA** *takes a long sip.)*

VERONICA. I don't see what the big deeeAHAHA HAAAGHAMN!
(Brain freeze.) Son of a bitch!

(They both crack up. **CHANDLER** *enters.)*

CHANDLER. Veronica!

VERONICA. I gotta go.

J.D. So I see.

CHANDLER. Corn Nuts?

VERONICA. Yes, Heather.

CHANDLER. Wave bye-bye to "Red Dawn" here and let's
motor.

[MUSIC NO. 04A "TRANSITION TO PARTY"]

*(***CHANDLER** *exits with* **VERONICA.** **J.D.** *hums and
disappears into the shadows as lights change...)*

J.D.
HMM... HMM...

Scene Five

(Ram's house. Suburban, upscale, very John Hughes. Lights up on **KURT** *and* **RAM** *getting lectured by their two* **DADS**. *Both men are rugged ex-jocks, dressed for a fishing trip.)*

RAM'S DAD. Okay, Ram. Have fun tonight, but I expect you to act your age. The Hendersons have the phone number for the cabin. If they call to complain, I'm gonna drive back here and knock the sand out of your diapers.

RAM. Dude! What am I, five?

RAM'S DAD. I'm your dad, not your dude.

KURT'S DAD. That goes double for you, Kurt. You're a guest in Bill's house and you will treat it with respect.

KURT. *(Smirking.)* Sure thing. *Dude.*

*(***RAM*** cracks up laughing. ***KURT'S DAD*** takes the challenge in stride, smiling. Then to ***RAM'S DAD***:)*

KURT'S DAD. Hold his arms.

*(***RAM'S DAD*** grabs ***KURT****'s arms.* ***KURT'S DAD*** puts his son in a headlock, laughing.)*

KURT'S DAD.	**KURT.**
Who's a great big sissy? Who's going to prom in a bright pink dress? Who's a sissy?	Hey, come on! This isn't funny! Ow! Okay, me! I'm a sissy. I'm a big fat sissy.

(The **DADS** *release* **KURT**.*)*

KURT'S DAD. Darn right. Enjoy your party, son.

RAM'S DAD. Punch it in.

(The **DADS** *punch it in and exit.)*

KURT. Man, that sucked.

RAM. Who cares? The parents are gone and I got my party slippers on!

[MUSIC NO. 05 "BIG FUN"]

(Lights change. We're in Ram's backyard.)

(TEEN PARTY GUESTS enter and dance. Note: This is a party for popular kids only. PREPPY is specifically scripted here, as is STONER [probably invited because she carries weed]. The rest of the PARTY GUESTS should be other members of the ensemble re-costumed as different, cooler characters.)

ALL.

NA-NA! NA-NA! NA NA-NA!
NA NA! NA! NA! NA! NA! NA-NA!

RAM.

DAD SAYS "ACT YOUR AGE."
YOU HEARD THE MAN,
IT'S TIME TO RAGE!

ALL.

BLAST THE BASS,
TURN OUT THE LIGHT!
AIN'T NOBODY HOME TONIGHT!

RAM.

DRINK, SMOKE, IT'S ALL COOL.
LET'S GET NAKED IN MY POOL!

ALL.

PUNCH THE WALL AND START A FIGHT,
AIN'T NOBODY HOME TONIGHT!

(KURT hits on CHANDLER.)

KURT.

HIS FOLKS GOT A WATER BED.
COME UPSTAIRS AND REST YOUR HEAD.

(RAM drapes his arms around DUKE and MCNAMARA.)

RAM.

LET'S RUB EACH OTHER'S BACKS
WHILE WATCHING PORN ON CINEMAX!

(The HEATHERS push them away.)

KURT & PARTY GUESTS.

AHHHH!

ALL.

THE FOLKS ARE GO-O-ONE!

ALTO GIRLS & GUYS.

IT'S TIME FOR BIG FUN!

GIRLS.

BIG FUN!

GUYS.	**GIRLS.**
WE'RE UP TILL DAWN,	UP TILL DAWN,

ALTO GIRLS & GUYS.

HAVING SOME BIG FUN!

GIRLS.

BIG FUN!

GUYS.

WHEN MOM AND DAD
FORGET

GIRLS.

TO LOCK THE LIQUOR CABINET,	TO LOCK THE LIQUOR CABINET,
IT'S BIG FUN!	
	BIG FUN!
BIG FUN! – WHOO!	BIG FUN! – WHOO!

(The **HEATHERS** *do tequila shots.* **MCNAMARA** *teaches* **VERONICA** *how to do a shot.)*

MCNAMARA. So it's salt, then shot, then lime. Very important to get the order right.

*(***VERONICA** *licks salt from her hand, slugs the shot, and sucks the lime perfectly.* **MCNAMARA** *claps excitedly.)*

MCNAMARA. You're a natural! Just like my mom.

*(***PREPPY STUD** *passes, smiles at* **VERONICA**.*)*

PREPPY. Veronica, looking good tonight.

VERONICA. Whoa.

A HOT GUY SMILED AT ME!

WITHOUT A TRACE OF
   MOCKERY!

OTHERS.
   BRAINIAC CLEANS UP ALL
      RIGHT!
   VERONICA IS HOT
      TONIGHT.

FREAKED! TWEAKED!
   HEAD'S A BLUR.
HOW DID I GET SO
   POPULAR?

   DON'T GET CLOSE, YOU
      MIGHT IGNITE!
   VERONICA IS HOT
      TONIGHT!

DREAMS ARE COMING
   TRUE,
WHEN PEOPLE LAUGH BUT
   NOT AT YOU!
I'M NOT ALONE, I'M NOT
   AFRAID!
I FEEL LIKE BONO AT LIVE
   AID!

   AHHHHH!
   THE HOUSE IS OU-OU-
      OURS,
   GUYS & ALTO GIRLS.

VERONICA & GIRLS.   IT'S TIME FOR BIG FUN!
   BIG FUN!

   GUYS.   **GIRLS.**
      LET'S USE THEIR   USE THEIR
         SHOWERS,   SHOWERS,
                ALTO GIRLS.
      THAT SOUNDS LIKE   THAT SOUNDS LIKE
         BIG FUN!   BIG FUN!

VERONICA.   **GIRLS.**
   BIG FUN! **GUYS & GIRLS.**   BIG FUN!
             CRACK OPEN ONE
             MORE CASE!

(VERONICA observes a couple making out.)

VERONICA.

I THINK THAT'S WHAT THEY CALL "THIRD BASE."

GUYS.

BIG FUN!

VERONICA & GIRLS.

BIG FUN!

GUYS & GIRLS.

BIG FUN!

VERONICA.

I'M ACTUALLY HAVING

VERONICA.		**GUYS.**
BIG FUN!	**GIRLS.**	BIG FUN!
	BIG FUN!	
BIG FUN!	BIG FUN!	BIG FUN!
WHOO!	WHOO!	WHOO!

(KURT holds up a papier-mâché piñata. It's an adorable pig mascot wearing a sign that says "JEFFERSON RAZORBACKS.")

KURT. Yo, Rottweilers! What is Westerberg gonna do to the Razorbacks at Sunday's game?

RAM. Gonna make 'em go –

(He mimes sex with the piñata.)

(Pig squeals of pain.) WHEE! WHEE! WHEE! WHEE!

DUKE & STUDENTS.

AHHHHH THE PARTY'S HOT, HOT, HOT!

IT'S TIME FOR BIG FUN!

VERONICA & GIRLS.

BIG FUN!

(KURT hands a little cup to the passing VERONICA.)

KURT.

YOU NEED A JELLO SHOT!

GUYS & ALTO GIRLS.

WE'RE HAVING BIG FUN!

VERONICA & GIRLS.

BIG FUN!

(**VERONICA** *takes a jello shot, missing the arrival of* **MARTHA,** *looking horribly out of place.* **MARTHA** *carries a bottle of sparkling cider tied with a lovely ribbon.*)

(*The* **HEATHERS** *watch from across the room.*)

CHANDLER.

MARTHA DUMPTRUCK, IN THE FLESH.

DUKE.

HERE COMES THE COOTIE SQUAD. WE SHOULD –

CHANDLER.

SHUT UP, HEATHER!

DUKE.

SORRY, HEATHER!

MCNAMARA.

LOOK WHO'S WITH HER – OH, MY GOD!

(*She points to* **VERONICA** *approaching* **MARTHA.**)

HEATHERS.

DANG! DANG! DIGGETY-DANG-A-DANG!
DANG! DANG! DIGGETY-DANG-A-DANG!

(*They watch* **VERONICA** *with* **MARTHA.**)

VERONICA. I can't believe you actually came.

MARTHA. It's exciting, right? Excuse me, I want to say hello to Ram. I brought sparkling cider.

(*She moves off, passing the* **HEATHERS.**)

CHANDLER.

SHOWING UP HERE TOOK SOME GUTS.
TIME TO RIP 'EM OUT.

(**DUKE** *holds up the pig piñata, which* **KURT** *and* **RAM** *have abandoned.*)

DUKE.

WELL, WHO'S THIS PIG REMIND YOU OF?
ESPECIALLY THE SNOUT!

CHANDLER.

HAH!

HEATHERS.

DANG! DANG! DIGGETY-DANG-A-DANG!

DANG! DANG! DIGGETY-DANG-A-DANG!

(The **HEATHERS** *exit with the piñata.* **MARTHA** *approaches* **RAM** *and hands him the bottle of sparkling cider.)*

MARTHA. Hi, Ram. I wasn't gonna come, but since you took the trouble to write that sweet note...

RAM. What note? Why do you gotta be so weird all the time? People wouldn't hate you so much if you acted normal.

(He swigs some cider, makes a face.)

There's no alcohol in here! Are you trying to poison me?

(He exits. The **HEATHERS** *enter.* **DUKE** *has the piñata, but we don't get a good look at it yet.)*

HEATHERS & OTHERS.

DANG! DANG! DIGGETY-DANG-A-DANG!

DANG! DANG! DIGGETY-DANG-A-DANG!

DANG! DANG! DIGGETY-DANG-A-DANG!

DIGGETY-DANG-A-DANG!

THE FOLKS ARE GO-O-ONE,

ALTO GIRLS & GUYS.

IT'S TIME FOR BIG FUN!

GIRLS.

BIG FUN!

GUYS.	**GIRLS.**
WE'RE UP TILL DAWN	UP TILL DAWN,

ALTO GIRLS & GUYS.

HAVING SOME BIG FUN!

GIRLS.

BIG FUN!

KURT, RAM & GUYS.

SO LET THE SPEAKERS BLOW,

ALL.

THEY'LL BUY ANOTHER STEREO!

KURT, RAM & GUYS.

OUR FOLKS GOT NO CLUE

ALL.

'BOUT HALF THE SHIT THEIR CHILDREN DO!
WHY ARE THEY SURPRISED?
WHENEVER WE'RE UNSUPERVISED, IT'S

KURT, RAM & GUYS.

BIG FUN!

GIRLS.

BIG FUN!

GUYS.

BIG FUN!

GIRLS.

BIG FUN!

GUYS.

BIG FUN!

ALL.

BIG FUN! WHOOOO!

(Song ends. **CHANDLER** *whistles for attention.)*

[MUSIC NO. 05A "PIÑATA OF DOOM"]

CHANDLER. Okay, Westerbergers! Time to celebrate our upcoming victory over the Razorbacks by whacking apart their mascot!

*(***MCNAMARA*** *holds up a pillowcase and a baseball bat.)*

MCNAMARA. We need a volunteer to take the first swing at the piñata –

CHANDLER. – Martha Dunnstock! I think you should do the honors.

*(***VERONICA*** *immediately snaps to attention. This can't be good.)*

(Now everyone's looking at **MARTHA.** *She's nervous, too.)*

MARTHA. I don't really know this game.

MCNAMARA. Let's show this girl some Westerberg spirit! Whoo!

(*The* **HEATHERS** *prompt applause. Everyone joins in.*)

ALL BUT VERONICA. Martha! Martha! Martha! Martha!

(**MARTHA** *has little choice but to take the bat and allow* **MCNAMARA** *to slip the pillowcase over her head and spin her around.*)

MCNAMARA. Bring out the piñata!

(**DUKE** *presents the pig piñata. We now see it has been crudely outfitted to resemble* **MARTHA**: *glasses, wig, and a sign reading "MARTHA DUMPTRUCK."*)

VERONICA. What is your damage, Heather?!

(*She grabs the piñata from* **DUKE** *and walks away.*)

(**DUKE** *chases after her like a small, yappy dog.*)

DUKE. What do you think you're doing?! Come back here with that! Veronica, c'mon!

VERONICA. You want it? Swim for it.

(*She hurls the piñata into the swimming pool.*)

(*The party has come to a dead stop.*)

(**MARTHA** *removes the pillowcase from her head. She looks around, confused.*)

MARTHA. What's going on?

VERONICA. Go home. I'll explain later.
(*Emphatic.*) Go.

(**MARTHA** *exits.* **VERONICA** *turns to* **CHANDLER,** *who has remained aloof and unreadable through all this.*)

Well, we gave it a shot. I'm resigning my commission from the Lip Gloss Gestapo. Going back to civilian life.

(*She starts to walk away.* **CHANDLER** *stops her, spins her, and immobilizes.*)

CHANDLER. No!

VERONICA. Don't spin me, I'm not feeling well.

CHANDLER. You don't *get* to be a nobody. Come Monday, you're an ex-somebody. Not even the losers will touch you now.

(VERONICA pushes CHANDLER off. She's quite breathless and a little queasy.)

Transfer to Washington. Transfer to Jefferson. No one at Westerberg's going to let you play their reindeer games.

(Suddenly, VERONICA vomits all over CHANDLER.)

(CHANDLER shrieks.)

CHANDLER. Aaaagh! I raised you up from nothing. And what's my thanks? I got paid in puke!

VERONICA. Lick it up, baby. Lick. It. Up.

CHANDLER. I know who *I'm* eating lunch with on Monday. Do you?

(This hits VERONICA like a hammer. She looks around at the PARTY GUESTS, seeking an ally or a kind face. Every single kid looks away. The crowd parts, and VERONICA exits, wilting under CHANDLER's unwavering, baleful glare. Once CHANDLER is satisfied that her enemy has been vanquished, she turns back to the PARTY GUESTS and beams with peppy enthusiasm –)

Okay, party people! Where's the goddamned keg?!

(Everyone cheers. Party on! Lights change...)

[MUSIC NO. 05B "WHERE'S THE GODDAMN KEG"]

Scene Six

[MUSIC NO. 06 "DEAD GIRL WALKING"]

(VERONICA wanders the dark suburban street, alone and scared.)

VERONICA.

THE DEMON QUEEN OF HIGH SCHOOL HAS DECREED IT:
SHE SAYS MONDAY, EIGHT A.M., I WILL BE DELETED.
THEY'LL HUNT ME DOWN IN STUDY HALL;
STUFF AND MOUNT ME ON THE WALL.
THIRTY HOURS TO LIVE – HOW SHALL I SPEND THEM?

I DON'T HAVE TO STAY AND DIE LIKE CATTLE:
I COULD CHANGE MY NAME AND RIDE UP TO SEATTLE.
BUT I DON'T OWN A MOTORBIKE – WAIT…

(Lights up on J.D. reading in bed at home.)

HERE'S AN OPTION THAT I LIKE:
SPEND THOSE THIRTY HOURS GETTIN' FREAKAY!

YEAH!

I NEED IT HARD.
I'M A DEAD GIRL WALKIN'!
I'M IN YOUR YARD.
I'M A DEAD GIRL WALKIN'!
BEFORE THEY PUNCH MY CLOCK,
I'M SNAPPIN' OFF YOUR WINDOW LOCK.
GOT NO TIME TO KNOCK,
I'M A DEAD GIRL WALKIN'!

(She climbs into J.D.'s window.)

J.D. Veronica? What are you doing in my room?

VERONICA.

HAD TO SEE YOU, HOPE I DIDN'T WAKE YOU.
SEE, I DECIDED I MUST RIDE YOU TILL I BREAK YOU.
'CAUSE HEATHER SAYS I GOTS TO GO.
YOU'RE MY LAST MEAL ON DEATH ROW.
SHUT YOUR MOUTH AND LOSE THEM TIGHTY-WHITAYS!
COME ON!

> TONIGHT I'M YOURS.
> I'M YOUR DEAD GIRL WALKIN'!
> GET ON ALL FOURS.
> KISS THIS DEAD GIRL WALKIN'!
> LET'S GO, YOU KNOW THE DRILL...
> I'M HOT AND PISSED AND ON THE PILL.
> BOW DOWN TO THE WILL OF A DEAD GIRL WALKIN'!
>
> AND YA KNOW, YA KNOW, YA KNOW,
> IT'S 'CAUSE YOU'RE BEAUTIFUL.
> YOU SAY YOU'RE NUMB INSIDE...
> BUT I CAN'T AGREE.
> SO THE WORLD'S UNFAIR...
> KEEP IT LOCKED OUT THERE.
> IN HERE IT'S BEAUTIFUL...
> LET'S MAKE THIS BEAUTIFUL!

J.D. That works for me.

(They make out.)

VERONICA.

> YEAH! FULL STEAM AHEAD!
> TAKE THIS DEAD GIRL
>   WALKIN'!

J.D.

> HOW'D YOU FIND MY
>   ADDRESS?

> LET'S BREAK THE BED!
> ROCK THIS DEAD GIRL
>   WALKIN'!
> NO SLEEP TONIGHT FOR YOU,
> BETTER CHUG THAT
>   MOUNTAIN DEW.

> I THINK YOU TORE MY
>   MATTRESS!

> OKAY, OKAY!

> GET YOUR ASS IN GEAR,
> MAKE THIS WHOLE TOWN
>   DISAPPEAR.

> OKAY! OKAY!

> SLAP ME! PULL MY HAIR,
> TOUCH ME
> THERE AND THERE AND THERE
> BUT NO MORE TALKING!

> THERE! THERE! THERE!

J.D.

VERONICA.   WHOA, OA, OA, OA!
 LOVE THIS DEAD GIRL
  WALKIN'!   WHOA! WHOA!
           HEY! HEY!
           YEAH! YEAH!
 LOVE THIS DEAD GIRL   LOVE THIS DEAD GIRL –
  WALKIN'!   WHOA! WHOA!
           HEY! HEY!
           WAIT! WAIT!
 LOVE THIS DEAD GIRL –   LOVE THIS DEAD GIRL–
 YEAH!   YEAH!
 YEAH!   YEAH!
 YEAH!   YEAH!
           OW!
 YEAH!!   YEAH!!

(They fall into the bed. Song ends. Blackout.)

(Spotlight on imaginary CHANDLER, *wearing 3D glasses. She's watching* J.D. *and* VERONICA *sleep.)*

[MUSIC NO. 06A "VERONICA'S CHANDLER NIGHTMARE"]

CHANDLER. Hello, slut.

*(*VERONICA *sits up in bed, freaked out.)*

VERONICA.   SPOOKY TEENS.
How did you get in here?   HO...

(Lights reveal SPOOKY TEENS *somewhat incongruously wearing gospel robes and 3D glasses. Eerie choral vocals build in intensity under the following.)*

CHANDLER.   SPOOKY TEENS.
I'm like oxygen. I'm everywhere.   HO...
Really, Veronica, you slept with
that? I will crucify you on Monday.
Everyone's gonna know good   HO...
little Veronica Sawyer is nothing
but a dirty whore.

VERONICA. Why are you so determined to hurt me?

CHANDLER.	**SPOOKY TEENS.**
Because I can. It'll be so very.	HO...

SPOOKY TEENS.

VERY! VERY! VERY! VERY!
VERY! VERY! VERY! VERY!

(The choral voices build to a scary climax. **VERONICA** *screams. Lights change;* **CHANDLER** *and the* **SPOOKY TEENS** *exit in darkness.)*

*(***J.D.*** *sits up in bed to comfort* **VERONICA,** *who is shaking.)*

J.D. You okay? You're soaking wet.

VERONICA. It was just a dream.

(She jumps out of bed and gets dressed.)

J.D. What's the rush?

VERONICA. I've gotta get to Heather's house.

J.D. Why?! You said you were done with Heather.

VERONICA. Yeah, and it was a sweet fantasy. A world without Heather. A world where everyone is free. But now it's morning and I have to go kiss her aerobicized ass.

(She starts to exit.)

J.D. Let me come with.

VERONICA. Really?

J.D. For backup.

VERONICA. Okay, thanks.

(She kisses **J.D.***)*

VERONICA. By the way... *(Pats his chest.)* You were my first.

(Lights change...)

[MUSIC NO. 06AA "BEDTIME FOR CHANDLER"]

Scene Seven

(Chandler's house. Two playing areas – Chandler's bedroom and the kitchen. **CHANDLER** *is still in bed.)*

*(***VERONICA** *and* **J.D.** *enter the kitchen.)*

VERONICA. *(Calls out.)* Heather?

[MUSIC NO. 06B "DEATH AT DAWN"]

J.D. Maybe she's not here.

*(***VERONICA** *pulls out an egg and cracks it into a ceramic mug. Clearly she's done this before. Over the following,* **VERONICA** *pulls out bottles of Worcestershire sauce, vinegar, hot sauce and adds them to the mug.)*

VERONICA. Trust me. She skips the Sunday morning trip to Grandma's even when she's not hungover.
(Calls out.) Heather? Heather!

*(***CHANDLER** *bellows from her bedroom.)*

CHANDLER. What?!

VERONICA. It's Veronica. I'm here to apologize.

CHANDLER. Hope you brought kneepads, bitch. Fix me a prairie oyster and I'll think about it.

*(***J.D.** *uncaps a bottle and hands it to* **VERONICA.***)*

J.D. Don't forget the Worcestershire.

VERONICA. You know your hangover cures.

J.D. My dad taught me all kinds of stuff.

VERONICA. *(Suddenly inspired.)* Oh, hey, here's my revenge. I'm gonna drop a phlegm globber in her prairie oyster. She'll never know.

(She hocks a loogie and spits into the mug. **J.D.** *pulls out some drain cleaner.)*

J.D. I'm a "No Rust Build-up" man, myself.

VERONICA. Don't be a dick. That stuff'll kill her.

J.D. Thus ending her hangover. I say we go with Big Blue.

(He pours the drain cleaner into an identical ceramic mug.)

VERONICA. What are you doing? You can't just – Besides, she'd never drink anything that looks like that.

J.D. Ceramic mug, dim light, she won't know what she's drinking.

VERONICA. Forget it.

J.D. Chick-en.

VERONICA. You're not funny.

J.D. Okay, I'm sorry.

*(He kisses **VERONICA**, long and slow. The moment is broken by –)*

CHANDLER. Prairie oyster! Chop-chop!

*(**VERONICA** picks up the wrong mug.)*

J.D. *(Sees her mistake.)* Veronica – you…

VERONICA. *(Turning back.)* I what?

J.D. Good luck.

*(He follows as **VERONICA** cautiously approaches **CHANDLER** in the bedroom playing area.)*

VERONICA. Morning, Heather.

*(**CHANDLER** rouses herself.)*

CHANDLER. Ah, Veronica. And Jesse James. *Quelle surprise.* [Pronounced "KELL-sup-PREEZ."]

(She grabs the mug.)

Let's get to it. Beg.

VERONICA. We both said things we didn't mean last night.

CHANDLER. I actually would prefer you did this on your knees. In front of your boy-toy here.

VERONICA. Uh-huh. Anyhow, I'm really sorry –

CHANDLER. – Do I look like I'm kidding? Down.

*(**VERONICA** kneels, humiliated. **J.D.** looks away.)*

Nice. But you're still dead to me.

(She downs the mug.)

(Beat. She gags.)

CHANDLER. Corn Nuts!

(She sinks to her knees, choking, and dies. A long, terrible beat as **J.D.** *and* **VERONICA** *stare in shock.)*

J.D. *Quelle surprise*, indeed.

VERONICA. Don't just stand there! Call 911!

J.D. Little late for that.

VERONICA. Heather! Heather, wake up! Oh my God! I just killed my best friend.

J.D. And your worst enemy.

VERONICA. Same difference. The police are going to think I did this on purpose! They're gonna have to send my SAT scores to San Quentin!

J.D. Unless…

(He picks up a book.)

Look. She was reading *The Bell Jar.*

[MUSIC NO. 06C "PAIN IN MY PATH"]

VERONICA. Oh no.

J.D. Oh yes. You can fake her handwriting.

(He offers **VERONICA** *a pen.)*

Make her sound deep. Like this –
I HAD PAIN IN MY PATH,
LIKE SYLVIA PLATH.
MY PROBLEMS WERE MYRIAD…

VERONICA.
I WAS HAVING MY PERIOD…

(She giggles hysterically, more from panic than mirth. Her eyes return to **CHANDLER** *and back to reality.)*

Oh my God!

J.D. This isn't funny! You could go to jail! Get your head straight. Now!

VERONICA. Heather would never use the word "myriad," okay?! She missed it on her vocabulary quiz.

J.D. So it's a badge for her failures at school! Work with me.

VERONICA. Okay, okay.

(**VERONICA** *looks around, picks up a pad, concentrates.*)

What would she say? What is her final statement to a cold, uncaring planet?

[MUSIC NO. 07 "THE ME INSIDE OF ME"]

VERONICA. Dear world…
BELIEVE IT OR NOT, I KNEW ABOUT FEAR;
I KNEW THE WAY LONELINESS STUNG.
I HID BEHIND SMILES AND CRAZY HOT CLOTHES;
I LEARNED TO KISS BOYS WITH MY TONGUE.

J.D. That's good.

VERONICA.
BUT OH, THE WORLD IT HELD ME DOWN…
IT WEIGHED LIKE A CONCRETE PROM QUEEN CROWN.

(**DEAD CHANDLER** *sits up. Only* **VERONICA** *sees her.*)

DEAD CHANDLER.
NO ONE THINKS A PRETTY GIRL HAS FEELINGS.
NO ONE GETS HER INSECURITY.
I AM MORE THAN SHOULDER PADS AND MAKEUP.
NO ONE SEES THE ME INSIDE OF ME.

Jesus, you're making me sound like Air Supply.

J.D. Keep going. This has to be good enough to fool the cops.

(*Lights change. Two* **COPS,** **OFFICER MCCORD** *and* **OFFICER MILNER,** *enter and stand over the dead body.*)

MILNER. Is it murder?

(**MCCORD** *picks up the suicide note.*)

MCCORD. No, look. Here's a suicide note.

VERONICA, DEAD CHANDLER & MCCORD.
THEY COULDN'T SEE PAST MY ROCK STAR MYSTIQUE,
THEY WOULDN'T DARE LOOK IN MY EYES.

VERONICA, DEAD CHANDLER & MILNER.
BUT JUST UNDERNEATH WAS A TERRIFIED GIRL
WHO CLINGS TO HER PILLOW AND CRIES!

VERONICA, DEAD CHANDLER & COPS.
MY LOOKS WERE JUST LIKE PRISON BARS;
VERONICA & COPS.
THEY'VE LEFT ME A MYRIAD OF SCARS.
DEAD CHANDLER. *(Impressed.)* "Myriad." Nice.

(Lights change. We're back at school. The **COPS** *hand the suicide note to* **PRINCIPAL GOWAN,** *who is with* **COACH RIPPER** *and* **FLEMING.** *)*

VERONICA, DEAD CHANDLER & COPS.
NO ONE THINKS A PRETTY GIRL HAS SUBSTANCE.

THAT'S THE CURSE OF

VERONICA & DEAD CHANDLER.   **COPS.**
POPULARITY.   POPULARI– POPULARITY.

*(***PRINCIPAL GOWAN** *reads the note aloud.)*

PRINCIPAL GOWAN.
I AM MORE THAN JUST A SOURCE OF HANDJOBS.
VERONICA, DEAD CHANDLER, GOWAN & COPS.
NO ONE SEES THE ME INSIDE OF ME.

(The **COPS** *exit.)*

*(***DEAD CHANDLER** *lounges nearby, an interested observer.)*

COACH RIPPER. I'm tellin' you, Principal Gowan – Heather Chandler is not your everyday suicide. You should cancel classes.

PRINCIPAL GOWAN. No way, Coach. I send the kids home before lunch and the switchboard will light up like a Christmas tree.

MS. FLEMING. Our children are dying! What this school needs is a good old-fashioned rap session. I suggest we get everyone into the cafeteria and just talk. And feel. Together.

PRINCIPAL GOWAN. Thank you, Ms. Fleming. Call me when the shuttle lands.

*(***COACH RIPPER** *and* **PRINCIPAL GOWAN** *chuckle.* **MS. FLEMING** *shoots them both a dirty look.)*

MS. FLEMING. Go ahead, laugh at the hippy, but I'm telling you we all misjudged Heather Chandler! Myself included! Have you read this suicide note?! Really read it?

(MS. FLEMING and DEAD CHANDLER read aloud.)

MS. FLEMING & DEAD CHANDLER.
BOX UP MY CLOTHING FOR GOODWILL,
LET'S GIVE THE POOR A HELPING HAND.
DONATE MY NECKLACES AND RINGS
TO STARVING CHILDREN EATING SAND.
SEND THEM MY HATS AND MY CDS,
MY PUMPS, MY FLATS, MY THREE TVS!

(STUDENTS observe, aware that something big is going down. Some might try to eavesdrop and get a look at the suicide note.)

DEAD CHANDLER, FACULTY & SOME STUDENTS.
NO ONE THINKS THE PRETTY GIRL HAS FEELINGS;
BUT I WEEP FOR ALL I FAILED TO BE. (I FAILED TO BE.)
MAYBE I CAN HELP THE WORLD BY LEAVING.
MAYBE THAT'S THE ME INSIDE OF ME.

GOWAN. Aw, hell. Long weekend for everybody!

(The STUDENTS cheer. The FACULTY MEMBERS exit, except for MS. FLEMING, who stops the excited STUDENTS from leaving.)

MS. FLEMING. Not so fast, kids. They're refuelling the buses, which gives us a solid half-hour of healing.

(The STUDENTS groan.)

(MS. FLEMING passes around mimeographed copies of the fake suicide note.)

MS. FLEMING.	**STUDENTS.**
I want you all to study this suicide note so you can really feel Heather's anguish.	OOH!... OOH!...

MCNAMARA.
HER WORLD SEEMED LIKE A PERFECT PLACE...

MS. FLEMING. Go on!

HIPSTER DORK.

BUT FRIENDS AND TOYS HAD NO EFFECT!

MS. FLEMING. Feel!

YOUNG REPUBLICANETTE.

THAT'S WHY SHE PUNCHED ME IN THE FACE –

MS. FLEMING. Heal!

STUDENTS.

'CAUSE SHE WAS DESPERATE TO CONNECT!

(VERONICA snorts a laugh at the absurdity of all this.)

MS. FLEMING. Veronica? Something on your mind?

(VERONICA quickly converts her laughter into a fake-sob.)

VERONICA. I'm sorry. It's just, this classroom discussion has stirred up emotions I haven't felt since Hands Across America.

MS. FLEMING. My God.

LOOK WHAT WE'VE DONE, WE'RE BREAKING THROUGH!
HEATHER WOULD BE SO PROUD OF YOU!

STUDENTS.

AND YOU! AND YOU! AND YOU! AND YOU!

MS. FLEMING & STUDENTS.

NO ONE THINKS A PRETTY GIRL CAN TOUCH YOU...

KURT & RAM. Heather touching me.

(KURT and RAM punch it in.)

MS. FLEMING & STUDENTS.

BUT SHE'S MADE US BETTER THAN WE WERE.
HEATHER'S DEAD, BUT SHE WILL LIVE INSIDE ME.
AND I'LL BE THE ME INSIDE OF HER...

DEAD CHANDLER. Holy crap! This is awesome!

MS. FLEMING & STUDENTS.

HEATHER CRIED; OUR SINS FELL ON HER SHOULDERS.

DEAD CHANDLER. Jesus Christ!

MS. FLEMING & STUDENTS.

HEATHER DIED, SO WE COULD ALL BE FREE!

DEAD CHANDLER. I'm bigger than John Lennon!

MS. FLEMING & STUDENTS.

HEATHER'S GONE, BUT SHE WILL LIVE FOREVER!

MARTHA.

SHE'S THE DOVE THAT SINGS OUTSIDE MY WINDOW!

BELEAGUERED GEEK.

SHE'S THE TWIN FROM WHOM I'M SEPARATED!

STONER CHICK.

SHE'S THE HORSE I NEVER GOT FOR CHRISTMAS!

MS. FLEMING & STUDENTS.

HEATHER SEES THE ME INSIDE OF ME!

DEAD CHANDLER, MS. FLEMING & STUDENTS.

HEATHER IS THE ME INSIDE OF ME!

INSIDE OF ME!

(Blackout. Lights change.)

[MUSIC NO. 07A "THE ME INSIDE OF ME PLAYOFF"]

Scene Eight

(J.D.'s living room. Unpacked moving boxes. **VERONICA** *and* **J.D.** *watch* **MS. FLEMING** *being interviewed on TV. She's emotional.)*

MS. FLEMING. As anyone who saw *The Breakfast Club* can tell you, all teenagers are essentially the same. Heather was not alone in feeling alone.

*(***DUKE*** *"camera bombs"* **MS. FLEMING.** *She mugs and waves to the camera.* **MS. FLEMING** *attempts to block her.)*

She wanted to love everything and everyone, but something stopped her. We have to identify the other ticking bombs out there.

*(***MS. FLEMING*** *shoves* **DUKE** *offstage.)*

Identify and heal them.

(Choking up.) I gave Heather a C-minus last week and now I lie awake at night wondering...

VERONICA. God, turn it off!

MS. FLEMING. ...Is that what set her over the edge?

*(***J.D.*** *remote-clicks off the TV. Lights out on* **MS. FLEMING.** *)*

VERONICA. I'm tired of watching this crap. Shows like this make suicide look cool. "Hey kids, make your teacher cry, get the respect you didn't get in life." It's gross.

(Beat.)

Do you think Heather's mother will keep everything in her room the same, like she's alive?

J.D. Well, that rug's gonna need a good cleaning. Why?

VERONICA. I feel bad. She was a human being and we killed her.

(Beat.)

You feel bad too, right?

J.D. Of course.

(We hear the front door open and close. **J.D.** *jumps to his feet, slightly panicked.)*

You want some ice cream? Let's go hit Dairy Queen.

VERONICA. What's wrong?

BIG BUD. *(Offstage.)* Jason?

J.D. We need to leave, now.

VERONICA. What's going on?

BIG BUD. *(Offstage.)* Jason? You here?

J.D. It's my dad.

VERONICA. Cool, I wanna meet him.

J.D. Not a good idea.

*(**BIG BUD DEAN** enters in a hurry. He exudes skeevy menace.)*

BIG BUD. Jason! Showtime!

*(**VERONICA** jumps up to shake his hand.)*

VERONICA. Mr. Dean, hello.

*(**BIG BUD** just stares at her.)*

J.D. Veronica, this is my dad. Big Bud Dean…

BIG BUD. *(Interrupting.)* Get rid of her.

(He rifles through a small stack of fake driver's licenses as he speaks.)

Some friends of ours need a hotel brought down. Run over to Sears, pick up eighty pounds of fertilizer and some diesel fuel. Use the Nevada I.D.

(He offers a license to **J.D.**, *who refuses to take it.)*

J.D. *(Defiant.)* I'm going out for ice cream with my girlfriend.

*(**BIG BUD** chuckles mirthlessly.)*

BIG BUD. You know how I'd blow up one of these shitbox suburban houses? Pack the top floor with thermals, set it all off with a Norwegian in the boiler room.
*(To **VERONICA**, pointed, a threat to his son.)* Where's your house, sweetheart?

(An ugly pause.)

VERONICA. I should go. My mom's expecting me for dinner. Spaghetti with lots of oregano.

J.D. Nice. The last time I saw my mom, she was waving out the window of a library in Texas. Right, Dad?

*(**BIG BUD** smiles at **J.D.** with malice.)*

BIG BUD. Right, *son.*

VERONICA. Okay, well… See you tomorrow.

(She hurries out. Blackout on J.D.'s house.)

[MUSIC NO. 07B "TRANSITION TO LEHMANN'S FARM"]

VERONICA. Dear Diary: J.D.'s dad will *not* be speaking at our wedding.

*(A phone rings. **VERONICA**, now at home, picks up the receiver.)*

Hello?

*(Lights up on **MCNAMARA** talking on a pay phone. **DUKE** is with her.)*

MCNAMARA. Veronica, I need help. I'm out at Lehmann's Farm.

VERONICA. What's wrong?

MCNAMARA. Just hurry up – please! It's an emergency.

*(Lights down on **MCNAMARA** as she hangs up. **VERONICA** hangs up, puzzled. Lights change as **VERONICA** crosses to…)*

enter downstage right (handwritten)

Scene Nine

↑ right (handwritten)

(A cow pasture. **DUKE** *and* **MCNAMARA** *pick their way through the muddy pasture, lifting their shoes, generally grossed out. The following optional dialogue may be used to cover the scene change:)*

DUKE. Is she coming?

MCNAMARA. She said she was. I kinda feel bad dragging her all the way out here.

DUKE. No one cares about your feelings. Ugh, this mud's gonna ruin my shoes.

MCNAMARA. I'm not sure it's mud. → stop (handwritten)

DUKE. Shit!

MCNAMARA. Exactly.

(End optional dialogue.)

*(***VERONICA*** *approaches* **DUKE** *and* **MCNAMARA***.)*

VERONICA. What are you two doing in the middle of a cow pasture?

DUKE. We're stranded.

MCNAMARA. We thought we were headed to the cemetery to pour a jug of Thunderbird on Heather's grave, y'know from her homies, but Kurt and Ram saw cows and stopped the car.

*(***MCNAMARA*** *points offstage, some distance away.* **VERONICA** *looks where she's pointing.)*

VERONICA. Why? There's nothing out here but –

RAM. *(Offstage.)* Okay, man. Put your back into it.

KURT. *(Offstage.)* Count of three.

VERONICA. *(Looking offstage.)* What are they doing?

DUKE. Cow-tipping.

KURT. *(Offstage.)* One…two…

RAM & KURT. *(Offstage.)* Three!

(We hear an angry offstage "MOOOOOO!" then a THUD. Excited "woo-hoos" and such from RAM and KURT.)

DUKE. So immature.

(VERONICA turns back to the HEATHERS. She pulls out her car keys and twirls them on her finger.)

VERONICA. C'mon, I'll drive you guys home.

DUKE. That's not why we called you. We made a deal with the guys. → counterband veronica

VERONICA. Deal? What kind of deal?

MCNAMARA. If we got you to show up here, Kurt promised to give us his car keys so Heather and I could go home.

VERONICA. Show up for what exactly?

MCNAMARA. C'mon, I've seen you looking at Kurt.

VERONICA. What?

MCNAMARA. You think he's cute, right?

VERONICA. No.

MCNAMARA. And Ram? Also very cute.

VERONICA. No!

(RAM and KURT enter, drunk and jolly.)

KURT. The cows are down for the count!

RAM. And the chicks are up for grabs!

DUKE. Veronica's here so we're leaving. Car keys. Now.

KURT. Yeah, yeah. All right.

(He tosses DUKE the car keys.)

VERONICA. Oh no. No, no, no. → grab veronica

MCNAMARA. Have fun!

DUKE. Don't do anything we wouldn't do!

(DUKE and MCNAMARA exit. VERONICA tries to follow, but KURT grabs her keys from her hand and tosses them to RAM. A game of "keep-away" ensues.)

VERONICA. Come on, give me my keys.

(She jumps for her keys, getting frustrated.)

Stop screwing around. I have to get home!

(Both **JOCKS** *are smiling, but there is a faint whiff of menace here.* **VERONICA** *is getting scared.)*

KURT. Oh no, you can't just leave.

[MUSIC NO. 08 "YOU'RE WELCOME"]

*(***VERONICA***'s keyring is attached to a blue scrunchie.* **KURT** *slips it over his wrist.)*

RAM. Not when you're dressed like that.

*(***VERONICA*** *evaluates her own outfit. It's her normal Heathers-approved attire.)*

VERONICA. Dressed like what? That is what I always wear.

KURT. Yeah! And it's torture.

RAM. How can you expect us to control ourselves when you look like that?

(The **JOCKS** *advance.* **VERONICA** *is acutely aware that she's alone and vulnerable.* **KURT** *and* **RAM** *freeze as* **VERONICA** *thinks to herself.)*

VERONICA.
DEAR DIARY:
HERE WE ARE IN THE DARK, FIFTY YARDS FROM MY CAR.
I COULD CLIMB THAT TREE –
(Reconsidering.) I'D NEVER GET THAT FAR.
THEY'RE A HUNDRED POUNDS HEAVIER, THEY HAVE MY KEYS.
I'M A RAT IN A TRAP. CORRECTION – I'M THE CHEESE.

*(***RAM** *makes a move toward* **VERONICA**. **KURT** *pushes* **RAM** *away.)*

KURT.
HEY THERE, GIRL, IGNORE THIS FOOL.
KURT.
HE TRIES TO PLAY COOL,
WHILE HE'S DRIBBLIN' DROOL.
RAM.
JUS' TRYIN' TO SAY IN OUR FRIENDLY WAY
THAT YOU'VE GOTTEN HOTTER LIKE EVERY DAY.

(He pushes **KURT** *away.)*

KURT.

OW!!

RAM.

HEY THERE, GIRL, AVOID THIS PUNK.

HE'S HUNGRY FOR A HUNK

OF THE JUNK IN YOUR TRUNK.

KURT.

THERE IS NO LIE THAT DOG WON'T TRY

WHEN A TASTY TREAT LIKE YOU WALKS BY! 'CAUSE:

RAM & KURT.

ONCE YOU WERE GEEKY AND NERDAY.

NOW YOU'RE FLIRTY,

FREAKY AND DIRTAY.

KURT.

YOU WERE NOTHING, AND NOBODY,

RAM.

BUT NOW YOU'RE GOOD ENOUGH TO –

RAM & KURT.

GET WITH ME!

HUH!

RAM, KURT & OFFSTAGE DUDE VOICES.

YOU'RE WELCOME!

RAM & KURT.

LOOK WHERE YOU ARE!

RAM, KURT & OFFSTAGE DUDE VOICES.

YOU'RE WELCOME!

RAM & KURT.

YOU'VE WON THE FOOTBALL STAR!

RAM, KURT & OFFSTAGE DUDE VOICES.

YOU'RE WELCOME!

RAM.

BABY, WHAT'S THAT SMELL?

KURT.

THAT'S THE SMELL OF ME LOVING YOU WELL!

RAM, KURT & OFFSTAGE DUDE VOICES.

YOU'RE WELCOME!

*(**RAM** and **KURT** beatbox. They freeze as **VERONICA** plots her next move.)*

VERONICA.

THIS IS NOT A DRILL, THIS IS NOT A BAD DREAM.
IN A COW PASTURE, NO ONE CAN HEAR YOU SCREAM.
NEVER BREAK THEIR STARE, STAY AWAKE, STAY AWARE.
YOU'RE NOT IN REAL DANGER
TILL THEY GRAB YOUR HAI-IIIIAAAAGH!

*(**RAM** and **KURT** paw at **VERONICA**'s hair. She takes hasty evasive action as **KURT** and **RAM** continue to compete for her attention, pushing each other, etc.)*

RAM.

COME BACK, GIRL, NOW DON'T PLAY HURT.
IF YOU DON'T WANT ME STARIN',
WHY YOU WEARIN' THAT SKIRT?

KURT.

WE CAN'T BE TAMED,
AND WE CAN'T BE BLAMED.
IT'S ALL YOUR FAULT THAT WE'RE INFLAMED! 'CAUSE

RAM & KURT.

ONCE YOU WERE GRODY AND GROTTY,

RAM.

NOW YOU GOT A BODY LIKE A MASERATI.

RAM & KURT.

STROKE MY FUR,
MAKE ME PURR.

KURT.

HEY, YOU WANTED TO BE

RAM, KURT & OFFSTAGE DUDE VOICES.

POPULAR!

KURT.

HIT ME!

*(**RAM** hits **KURT**.)*

HUH!

RAM, KURT & OFFSTAGE DUDE VOICES.

YOU'RE WELCOME!

RAM & KURT.

LOOK WHERE YOU ARE!

RAM, KURT & OFFSTAGE DUDE VOICES.

YOU'RE WELCOME!

RAM & KURT.

COME GETCHA FOOTBALL STAR!

RAM, KURT & OFFSTAGE DUDE VOICES.

YOU'RE WELCOME!

RAM.

COME JOIN THE PROS!

KURT.

ONCE WE SQUEEZE YOU, YOU'LL STAY SQUOZE!

RAM.

YOU'RE WELCOME IN MY LAP, WELCOME ON MY KNEE!

KURT.

WELL, COME ON AND GET GRABBY IN THE GRASS WITH ME!

(KURT and RAM freeze.)

VERONICA.

I GOT ONE LAST CHANCE TO SAVE MY ASS.

WHAT WAS THAT MOVE FROM SELF-DEFENSE CLASS?

(KURT and RAM advance on her.)

KURT.

I'LL STEAL YOUR HEART LIKE A THIEF,

RAM.

GIVE YOU SWEET RELIEF.

KURT.

CALL ME WENDY 'CAUSE YOU'LL NEVER WONDER

RAM & KURT.

"WHERE'S THE BEEF!"

(They freeze.)

VERONICA.

THEY'RE A POWDER KEG,

SO DON'T YELL OR BEG.

STAY FRIENDLY, THEN GENTLY,
"ACCIDENT'LLY," SWEEP THE LEG.

*(She sweeps **RAM**'s leg; he goes down, taking **KURT** with him. They wind up in the mud, stuck and messy.)*

RAM. This mud stinks!

KURT. Gross!

VERONICA.

YOU'RE WELCOME!

*(**KURT** sniffs **RAM**, makes a face.)*

KURT.

BACK UP, FOOL, YOU REEK!

VERONICA.

YOU'RE WELCOME.

*(**RAM** sniffs **KURT**, makes a face.)*

KURT.

WELL, YOU SMELL LIKE A SEWAGE LEAK!

VERONICA.

YOU'RE WELCOME.

KURT. *(It's dawning on him.)*

WAIT, DUDE, I'M PRETTY SURE…
THIS AIN'T MUD, IT'S –

RAM & KURT. *(Simultaneously horrified.)*

COW MANURE!

VERONICA & OFFSTAGE DUDE VOICES.

YOU'RE WELCOME!

RAM & KURT.

AAGGHHH! IT'S EVERYWHERE!

VERONICA & OFFSTAGE DUDE VOICES.

YOU'RE WELCOME!

RAM & KURT. *(Inspecting themselves.)*

OH GOD, IT'S IN MY HAIR!

VERONICA & OFFSTAGE DUDE VOICES.

YOU'RE WEL–

RAM & KURT.

HEY, GIRL, LET'S NOT DWELL –

KURT.

    ON THE SMELL –

RAM.

    YOU CAN TELL –

KURT, RAM & OFFSTAGE DUDE VOICES.

    I CAN STILL BE LOVIN' YOU WELL!

VERONICA.

    SWELL.

KURT. *(Shoving* **RAM***, competitive.)*

    NO,

KURT & OFFSTAGE DUDE VOICES.

    I'LL BE LOVIN' HER WELL.

VERONICA.

    SEE YOU IN HELL!

    *(***RAM*** and ***KURT*** are busy arguing, pushing and slap-
    fighting.)*

RAM.

    NO,

RAM & OFFSTAGE DUDE VOICES.

    I'LL BE LOVIN' HER WELL!

KURT.

    NO,

KURT & OFFSTAGE DUDE VOICES.

    I'LL BE

RAM & OFFSTAGE DUDE VOICES.

    I'LL BE!

KURT & OFFSTAGE DUDE VOICES.

    I'LL BE!

RAM & OFFSTAGE DUDE VOICES.

    I'LL BE!

RAM, KURT & OFFSTAGE DUDE VOICES.

    LOVIN' LOVIN' LOVIN' LOVIN' LOVIN' HER WELL!

VERONICA, RAM, KURT & OFFSTAGE DUDE VOICES.

    YOU'RE WELCOME!

    YOU'RE WELCOME!

    YOU'RE WELCOOOOOOME!

(VERONICA retrieves her car keys from KURT's wrist as he and RAM slip and fall into the manure again. Song ends. Blackout.)

Scene Ten

(VERONICA *writes in her diary.*)

[MUSIC NO. 08A "GHOST HEATHER"]

VERONICA. That was a close call. My so-called friends avoided date rape by volunteering me for date rape.

DEAD CHANDLER. That sort of assholery never happened when I was in charge.

(**DEAD CHANDLER** *steps out from the shadows.* **VERONICA** *is less than thrilled to see her.*)

VERONICA. Oh. You.

DEAD CHANDLER. I kept Ram and Kurt on a tight leash.

VERONICA. Look, I'm sorry you're dead and all, but let's not rewrite history. You were a thug.

DEAD CHANDLER. Maybe...

(*Lights change as they cross the stage. We're now back in high school, the next morning.*)

But I made the trains run on time. Everyone knew their place. The yearbook got done properly, the prom was consistently awesome and the Spirit Float always won a goddamn blue ribbon. Once you've scarfed down a hot bowl of chaos you'll look back on my regime as the good ol' days.

(**DEAD CHANDLER** *notices* **DUKE** *and* **MCNAMARA** *emptying the contents of a locker into a box.*)

What are those two pillowcases doing?

VERONICA. Looks like they're cleaning out your locker.

(**DUKE** *finds Chandler's signature red scrunchie. She holds it up, admires it.*)

MCNAMARA. Hey – that's Heather's scrunchie.

DUKE. Heather Chandler is gone. It's up to me to take her place.

MCNAMARA. Is...that a joke?

DEAD CHANDLER. Oh, it is most definitely a joke.

(**DUKE** *bristles at* **MCNAMARA**.)

DUKE. Why would you say that, Heather?

DEAD CHANDLER. See? Chaos.

DUKE. Because I'm not a cheerleader like you? You think you're better than me?

MCNAMARA. *(Flustered.)* What? No! It's just, Heather was our friend. We can't just swap her out like a lightbulb. I mean – that is –
(Nervously laughing.) – Shut up, Heather!

[MUSIC NO. 09 "NEVER SHUT UP AGAIN"]

DUKE. No, Heather. *You* shut up!

(**DUKE** *affixes the red scrunchie to her own hair.*)

I have a new favorite color!
HEATHER CHOKED.
BOUGHT THE FARM.
SHE COULD NOT HACK IT.
NOW WE NEED A STRONG ARM
TO RUN THIS RACKET.

HEATHER'S OUT.
WHO WILL RISE?
GOTTA FILL THAT VACUUM.
IT'S MY TURN.
IT'S MY PRIZE.
I SPIT LIGHTNING!

DUKE & STUDENTS.
CRACK!
BOOM!

DUKE.
I BIT MY TONGUE SO LONG.
I LEARNED TO COUNT TO TEN.
MY SILENCE MADE ME STRONG.
I DID MY TIME, AND THEN –
A HOUSE DROPPED

DUKE & STUDENTS.

ON HER HEAD,
THE WITCH IS DEAD!
DING DONG!

(DUKE shoves VERONICA aside, much like she was shoved aside earlier by Chandler.)

DUKE.

MOVE, BITCH, THIS MY SONG!

(With a flash! DUKE's outfit instantly transforms from her accustomed green to fierce Heather Chandler red!)

DUKE & STUDENTS.

I WILL NEVER SHUT UP AGAIN!
I WILL NEVER SHUT UP AGAIN!
BRAND-NEW DAY, WATCHING DREAMS COME TRUE!

DUKE.

WELL FOR ME, NOT YOU.

DUKE & STUDENTS.

'CAUSE I'LL
NEVER SHUT UP AGAIN!

(VERONICA, appalled by the spectacle, navigates around dancers, trying to avoid being trampled.)

DUKE.

GIRLS LIKE ME DON'T CLIMB HIGH.
CAN'T CRACK THAT CEILING.
BUT NOW I SCRAPE THE SKY.
IT'S YOU WHO'S KNEELING!
HEATHER'S PET, YOU'RE OLD NEWS.
LOOK AT YOU, YOU'RE BUSTED.
YOU THINK YOU'LL FILL HER SHOES?
TOO LATE I

DUKE & STUDENTS.

JUST DID!

(VERONICA manages to reach a safe spot. She writes in her diary, horrified.)

(DUKE addresses the other STUDENTS like she's Evita.)

DUKE.	STUDENTS.
NOW, I DON'T MEAN TO BRAG –	MEAN TO BRAG –
ONCE I WAS ONE OF YOU.	ONE OF YOU.
BUT NOW I AM THE FLAG	AM THE FLAG
YOU PLEDGE ALLEGIANCE TO.	'LEGIANCE TO.
I AM THE DREAM YOU CHASE.	DREAM YOU CHASE.
I'M YOUR AMAZING GRACE!	'MAZING GRACE!
YO, PARTY'S AT MY PLACE!	

(The **STUDENTS** *cheer.)*

STUDENTS.

WOO HOO!

DUKE & STUDENTS.

I WILL NEVER SHUT UP AGAIN!

I WILL NEVER SHUT UP AGAIN!

BRAND-NEW DAY!

NOW WE'RE FIN'LLY FREE –

DUKE. *(Lovingly, to the crowd.)*

FREE TO WORSHIP ME!

DUKE & STUDENTS.

'CAUSE I'LL NEVER SHUT UP –

*(***DUKE** *sees* **VERONICA** *is not participating. She holds up her hand for silence.)*

DUKE.

SHUT UP.

(The **STUDENTS** *obediently shut up.)*

*(***DUKE** *yanks the diary out of* **VERONICA***'s hands and starts yanking out pages.* **VERONICA** *freaks out, scrambling to recover her lost property.* **MCNAMARA** *helps recover pages too.)*

DON'T JUDGE ME,

LITTLE MISS INNOCENCE.

YOUR HANDS AIN'T CLEAN.

I'VE SEEN YOUR FINGERPRINTS.

DUKE.

YOU ACT SO UPTIGHT, SO VIRGIN WHITE –
BUT I HEARD FROM THE BOYS
WHAT YOU WERE UP TO LAST NIGHT!

(She snaps her fingers. **KURT** *and* **RAM** *step forward to testify.)*

KURT.

VERONICA'S MY WET DREAM!

RAM.

VERONICA LIKES TO SCREAM!

KURT.

VERONICA TOOK ONE FOR THE TEAM!

RAM.

SHE TOOK TWO FOR THE TEAM!

VERONICA. What?!

KURT & RAM.

THAT GIRL WAS ON HER BACK!

KURT, RAM & GUYS.

THAT GIRL WAS BIG FUN!

STUDENTS.

BIG FUN!

KURT & RAM.

WE SMOKED HER CRACK!

KURT, RAM & GUYS.

THAT CRACK WAS BIG FUN!

STUDENTS.

BIG FUN!

KURT, RAM & GUYS.

AND THAT'S WHEN THINGS WENT SOUTH –

KURT & RAM.

WE HAD A SWORDFIGHT IN HER MOUTH!

*(***KURT** *and* **RAM** *circle* **VERONICA,** *making obscene and mocking gestures. The* **STUDENTS** *enjoy the cruel spectacle, relieved it's not them in the spotlight.)*

DUKE & STUDENTS.	**KURT & RAM.**
WHOA!	OH!

STUDENTS.
DANG!
RAM, KURT & STUDENTS.
DIGGETY, DANG-A-DANG!
DUKE, KURT & RAM.
FREAK!

STUDENTS.	**VERONICA.**
DANG,	That's a lie!

RAM, KURT & STUDENTS.
DIGGETY, DANG-A-DANG!
DUKE, KURT & RAM.
SLUT!

STUDENTS.	
DANG,	Heather! Why?

KURT, RAM & STUDENTS.
DIGGETY, DANG-A-DANG!
DUKE, KURT, RAM & STUDENTS.
SWORDFIGHT IN HER MOUTH!

*(***VERONICA*** is hot with rage and humiliation. She screams.)*

VERONICA. Aagh!

DUKE & STUDENTS.	**KURT & RAM.**
I WILL NEVER SHUT UP AGAIN!	I WILL NEVER SHUT UP! SWORDFIGHT IN HER MOUTH
I WILL NEVER SHUT UP AGAIN!	I WILL NEVER SHUT UP! SWORDFIGHT IN HER MOUTH

DUKE, KURT, RAM & STUDENTS.
I'M ON FIRE AND YOU'RE MY FUEL.
DUKE. *(To* **VERONICA.***)*
YOU SHOULD FIND A NEW SCHOOL.

DUKE.	**KURT, RAM & STUDENTS.**
'CAUSE I'LL NEVER SHUT UP AGAIN!	'CAUSE I'LL NEVER SHUT UP AGAIN! NEVER SHUT UP AGAIN!
NO, NO, NO, NO, NO, NO, NO! ALL HAIL THE QUEEN. I WEAR THE RED.	NEVER SHUT UP AGAIN!

DUKE.	KURT, RAM & STUDENTS.
THE SCRUNCHIE'S ON MY HEAD!	NEVER SHUT UP AGAIN!
YOU CAN'T RUN!	
YOU CAN'T HIDE!	
I AM A CRIMSON TIDE!	NEVER SHUT UP AGAIN!
YOU BETTER MIND WHAT YOU DO:	
BIG SISTER'S WATCHING YOU!	NEVER SHUT UP AGAIN!
CAN I GET AN AMEN?	
	HEY!
'CAUSE I WILL NEVER SHUT UP AGAIN!	NEVER SHUT UP AGAIN!
HAH!	HAH!

*(Song ends. **J.D.** enters. He can tell something bad has happened, but he's not certain exactly what.)*

J.D. Veronica? What's wrong? What happened?

*(And that's when **VERONICA** bursts into tears. **KURT** laughs.)*

KURT. She cried just like that last night when she saw how big I was!

(Everyone laughs.)

RAM. Hell yeah, punch it in!

[MUSIC NO. 09A "J.D. GETS BEAT"]

*(Before they have a chance to bump fists, **J.D.** launches himself at **KURT**, pummelling him.)*

*(**RAM** and **PREPPY STUD** pull **J.D.** off **KURT** and throw him roughly to the floor. **J.D.**'s anger made him sloppy, and he's now lost the element of surprise.)*

Oh, you're dead now, pud-whacker.

*(**KURT**, **RAM**, and **PREPPY STUD** kick the crap out of **J.D.** The **STUDENTS** cheer with excitement.)*

*(**VERONICA** enters the melee, trying to help **J.D.**, but **RAM** backhands her without a second thought, sending her reeling.)*

(COACH RIPPER and PRINCIPAL GOWAN run in to break up the fight.)

COACH RIPPER. Nothing more to see here!

PRINCIPAL GOWAN. Get to class, all of you!

(PRINCIPAL GOWAN and COACH RIPPER drag KURT and RAM away, and the STUDENTS disperse.)

(VERONICA is left kneeling at J.D.'s side. They're alone and forgotten.)

[MUSIC NO. 10 "OUR LOVE IS GOD"]

VERONICA. You okay?

(J.D. nods, recovering.)

J.D. Sort of. What about you?

VERONICA. I'm fine. Awesome.

(But she's still trying to stop crying.)

Sorry about the waterworks.

J.D.

THEY MADE YOU CRY.
BUT THAT WILL END TONIGHT.
YOU ARE THE ONLY THING THAT'S RIGHT
ABOUT THIS BROKEN WORLD.
GO ON AND CRY,
BUT WHEN THE MORNING COMES,
WE'LL BURN IT DOWN AND THEN
WE'LL BUILD THE WORLD AGAIN...
OUR LOVE IS GOD.

(He looks away, self-conscious.)

VERONICA. Are you okay?

J.D.

I WAS ALONE.
I WAS A FROZEN LAKE.
BUT THEN YOU MELTED ME AWAKE;
SEE, NOW I'M CRYING TOO.

J.D.

YOU'RE NOT ALONE.   **VERONICA.**

                          YOU'RE NOT ALONE...

AND WHEN THE MORNING
    COMES,

                          WHEN THE MORNING
                              COMES...

WE'LL BURN AWAY THAT
    TEAR,
AND RAISE OUR CITY
    HERE...

                          RAISE OUR CITY HERE...
OUR LOVE IS GOD.   OUR LOVE IS GOD.

(Lights change. We're in J.D.'s bedroom. **J.D.** *watches* **VERONICA** *dial the phone.)*

(The phone rings in Kurt's house. **KURT** *answers,* **RAM** *listens in.)*

KURT. Yeah-lo?

VERONICA. Kurt...?

KURT. *(Pointedly, to alert* **RAM.***)* Hey! Veronica?

VERONICA. Sorry about the other night. I just couldn't decide which of you two hot gentlemen I wanted to be with. Then I realized, why decide at all?

KURT. Wait, what?

VERONICA. Meet me at the cemetery. At dawn.

KURT. Who? Me? Or Ram?

VERONICA. Yes.

(She hangs up.)

RAM. What'd she want?

KURT. Us!

RAM. No way!

KURT. Punch it in!

(Lights out on **KURT** *and* **RAM** *as they punch it in.)*

J.D.

WE CAN START AND FINISH WARS.

J.D. & VERONICA.

WE'RE WHAT KILLED THE DINOSAURS.

WE'RE THE ASTEROID THAT'S OVERDUE.

THE DINOSAURS CHOKED ON THE DUST;

THEY DIED BECAUSE GOD SAID THEY MUST.

THE NEW WORLD NEEDED ROOM FOR ME AND YOU.

J.D.

I WORSHIP YOU.

I'D TRADE MY LIFE FOR YOURS.

THEY ALL WILL DISAPPEAR,

WE'LL PLANT OUR GARDEN HERE...

VERONICA.

PLANT OUR GARDEN HERE...

J.D.

OUR LOVE IS GOD.

VERONICA.

OUR LOVE IS GOD.

J.D.

OUR LOVE IS GOD.

*(He opens a box and pulls out two World War II vintage Luger pistols. *VERONICA* flinches.)*

VERONICA. Whoa, are they real?

J.D. Yeah, but we're filling them with *ich luge* bullets.

VERONICA. *"Ich luge"*?

J.D. My granddad scored them in World War II. They contain a powerful tranquilizer. The Nazis used them to fake their own suicides when the Russians invaded Berlin. We'll knock out Ram and Kurt long enough to make it look like a suicide pact. Complete with a forged suicide note.

*(*FANTASY KURT* and *FANTASY RAM* enter.)*

FANTASY KURT & FANTASY RAM. "Ram and I died because we had to hide our gay forbidden love from a misapproving world."

(They exchange a loving look and exit, holding hands.)

J.D.

AND WHEN THE MORNING COMES,
THEY'LL BOTH BE LAUGHINGSTOCKS!

J.D. & VERONICA.

SO LET'S GO HUNT SOME JOCKS!

*(Lights change. It's dawn, out at the cemetery. **RAM** and **KURT** enter, excited and even a little nervous about the upcoming orgy. **RAM** wears a tie.)*

*(**VERONICA** is waiting for them.)*

KURT. *(A little bashful.)* Hi...Veronica.

RAM. Uh...so do we just whip it out or what?

VERONICA. Take it slow, Ram. Strip for me.

*(The **JOCKS** eagerly strip shirtless. **RAM** removes his tie.)*

Oh, I liked the tie.

*(**RAM** hastily reties the tie.)*

RAM. My mom bought it for me.

(They continue to strip down to their underpants.)

KURT. What about you?

VERONICA. I was hoping you'd rip my clothes off me, Sport. Count of three.

*(**KURT** and **RAM** stand awkwardly in their underpants. **RAM** giggles in anticipation.)*

VERONICA. One...two...

J.D. Three.

*(He steps out of hiding and nonchalantly shoots **RAM** dead. **VERONICA** fires awkwardly at **KURT**, missing him completely.)*

KURT. Aaaugh! Holy crap!

(He runs away.)

J.D. Don't move! I'll get him back!

(He runs after **KURT**.*)*

*(***VERONICA**, *suddenly worried, nudges the motionless* **RAM** *with her foot.)*

VERONICA. Ram? You're just unconscious, right? Ram? Ram!

*(***J.D.** *chases* **KURT**.*)*

KURT. *(Ad-lib as needed.)* Why are you chasing me? I was just kidding about your girlfriend being a whore!

(He tries to escape by scaling a fence.)

J.D. Off the damn fence! Get off the fence!

*(***KURT** *stops, halfway up. He turns back, exhausted and crying.)*

KURT. I don't understand!

J.D. *(Pointing gun.)*
WE CAN START AND FINISH WARS.
WE'RE WHAT KILLED THE DINOSAURS.
WE'RE THE ASTEROID THAT'S OVERDUE.

KURT. Stop being a dick!

J.D.
THE DINOSAURS WILL TURN TO DUST.

KURT. What does that *mean*?!

J.D.
THEY'LL DIE BECAUSE WE SAY THEY MUST.

(He shoots **KURT**, *who crumples to the ground, dead.* **VERONICA** *enters, horrified.)*

VERONICA. What the fuck have you done?!

(Beat. **J.D.** *looks at her and smiles with gentle certainty.)*

J.D.
I WORSHIP YOU.
I'D TRADE MY LIFE FOR YOURS.
WE'LL MAKE THEM DISAPPEAR.
WE'LL PLANT OUR GARDEN HERE.

*(***VERONICA** *sinks to her knees, stricken.* **J.D.** *kneels behind her.)*

J.D.

OUR LOVE IS GOD.
OUR LOVE IS GOD.   **OFFSTAGE VOICES.**
OUR LOVE IS GOD.   OOH!
OUR LOVE IS GOD.   OOH!
OUR LOVE IS GOD...   OOH!

(**J.D.** *gathers* **VERONICA** *into his arms. Either he doesn't notice her obvious horror, or he won't acknowledge it.* **VERONICA,** *overwhelmed by shock and dread, is powerless to break away.*)

VERONICA.   **OFFSTAGE VOICES.**

OUR LOVE IS GOD.   OHH!

J.D.

OUR LOVE IS GOD.

VERONICA.

OUR LOVE IS GOD.   OHH!

J.D.

OUR LOVE IS GOD...

AH! AHH!

(Blackout.)

ACT TWO

Scene One

[MUSIC NO. 10A "ORGAN ENTR'ACTE"]

(Entr'acte ends. In darkness:)

VERONICA. Dear Diary:

[MUSIC NO. 10B "PROM OR HELL?"]

(Lights up. A church. Two coffins have twin black football helmets resting atop them. **VERONICA** *enters, wearing black. She touches the coffins.)*

I'M GOING STEADY.
MOSTLY HE'S AWESOME,
IF A BIT TOO ROCK AND ROLL.
LATELY HE'S BUMPED OFF
THREE OF MY CLASSMATES.
GOD HAVE MERCY ON MY SOUL.
THEY WERE JUST SEVENTEEN.
THEY STILL HAD ROOM TO GROW.
THEY COULD HAVE TURNED OUT GOOD
BUT NOW WE'LL NEVER KNOW.

(Song ends. **J.D.** *enters, elegant in black.* **VERONICA** *is not thrilled to see him.)*

J.D. There's been a distinct lack of girls climbing through my bedroom window lately.

VERONICA. Take the hint.

J.D. Okay, you're mad. I get it.

VERONICA. No, I don't think you do. *"Ich luge"* bullets?! You lied to me!

J.D. You were lying to yourself. You wanted them dead too.

VERONICA. I did not!

J.D. Did too.

VERONICA. Did not!

J.D. Did too.

VERONICA. Did not!

J.D. Did they make you cry?

VERONICA. Yes.

J.D. Can they make you cry now?

VERONICA. No. But you can.

J.D. Just wait till you see the good that comes of this.

VERONICA. What good could possibly come of this?

J.D. Call me an optimist.

(He tries to kiss her cheek, but she turns her head slightly to avoid him.)

*(**MOURNERS** enter and take seats. Everyone wears black. The funeral is beginning. **J.D.** and **VERONICA** sit.)*

VERONICA. Dear Diary: My teenage angst bullshit has a body count.

*(**KURT'S DAD** gives a eulogy from a podium.)*

KURT'S DAD. I don't really know what I'm supposed to say up here. I'm ashamed, certainly. My family has turned our town into a laughingstock. My boy Kurt wasn't who I thought he was. When I think about the sick, disgusting things Kurt and Ram were doing...

*(**RAM'S DAD** rises from his seat.)*

RAM'S DAD. You wait just a minute, Paul!

*(Everyone turns to look. **RAM'S DAD** is uncomfortable with the attention. But grief and indignation press him on...)*

It is ignorant, hateful talk like yours that makes this world a place our boys could not live in!

[MUSIC NO. 11 "MY DEAD GAY SON"]

THEY WERE NOT DIRTY!
THEY WERE NOT WRONG!
THEY WERE TWO LONELY VERSES
IN THE LORD'S GREAT SONG!

KURT'S DAD.

OUR BOYS WERE PANSIES, BILL!

RAM'S DAD.

YES!
MY BOY'S A HOMOSEXUAL,
AND THAT DON'T SCARE ME NONE.
I WANT THE WORLD TO KNOW...
I LOVE MY DEAD GAY SON!

I've been thinking. Praying. Reading some magazines.
And it's time we opened our eyes.

WELL, THE GOOD LORD MADE GAY PENGUINS,
AND BONOBO CHIMPANZEES.
I'VE SEEN GAY LIONS SHOW THEIR PRIDE IN
    DOCUMENTARIES.
IF NATURE GETS HER ORDERS
HANDED DOWN FROM GOD ABOVE
THEN ANIMAL OR HUMAN,

RAM'S DAD.

YOU CAN'T HELP THE ONES
    YOU LOVE!

MOURNERS.

OO... WHOA... AH!

THEY WERE NOT DIRTY!

WHOA!

THEY WERE NOT FRUITS!

WHOA!

THEY WERE JUST
TWO STRAY LACES   OO...
IN THE LORD'S BIG BOOTS. WHOA!
WELL, I NEVER CARED
FOR HOMOS MUCH,
UNTIL I REARED ME ONE.
BUT NOW I'VE LEARNED TO   NOW...
    LOVE...   LEARNED TO LOVE...
I LOVE MY DEAD GAY SON!

MOURNERS.

HE LOVES HIS SON,
HE LOVES HIS SON,
HIS DEAD GAY SON!

RAM'S DAD.

NOW, I SAY MY BOY'S IN HEAVEN!
AND HE'S TANNING BY THE POOL.
THE CHERUBIM WALK HIM AND HIM,
AND JESUS SAYS IT'S COOL.
THEY DON'T HAVE CRIME OR HATRED,
THERE'S NO BIGOTRY OR CURSIN'.
JUST FRIENDLY FELLOWS DRESSED UP
LIKE THEIR

RAM'S DAD.	**MOURNERS.**
FAV'RITE VILLAGE PERSON!	OO… WHOA… AH!
THEY WERE NOT DIRTY –	
	NO, NO!
THEY JUST HAD FLAIR!	
	WHOA!
THEY WERE TWO	
BRIGHT RED RIBBONS	OO…
IN THE LORD'S LONG HAIR.	WHOA!
WELL, I USED TO SEE A HOMO	
AND GO REACHIN' FOR MY GUN.	
BUT NOW I'VE LEARNED TO LOVE…	NOW…LEARNED TO LOVE…
AND FURTHERMORE! –	

RAM'S DAD.

THESE BOYS WALKED HAND IN HAND!
THESE BOYS, THEY TOOK A STAND:
THEY COULD NOT WAIT
ONE SECOND LONGER TO BE FREE!
THEY CAST OFF THEIR DISGUISE,

NO SHAME, NO COMPROMISE!
PAUL, I CAN'T BELIEVE THAT YOU
STILL REFUSE TO GET A CLUE,

AFTER ALL THAT WE BEEN THROUGH!
I'M TALKING YOU AND ME.

MOURNERS. *(Gasping.)*

AH!

RAM'S DAD.

IN THE SUMMER OF '83.

MOURNERS. *(Gasping.)*

OHHH!

(KURT'S DAD stands, stunned for an awkward beat. Looks to the MOURNERS…then to RAM'S DAD.)

KURT'S DAD. That…was one hell of a fishing trip.

(He approaches RAM'S DAD. They kiss, overcome by relief and love.)

MOURNERS.

WHOA, WHOA, WHOA, WHOA,
WHOA! WHOA! WHOA!
THEY WERE NOT DIRTY!
WHOA!
AND NOT PERVERSE!
NO, NO!
THEY WERE TWO SHINING RHINESTONES
ON THE LORD'S BIG PURSE!

BOTH DADS.

OUR JOB IS NOW CONTINUING
THE WORK THAT THEY BEGUN!

KURT'S DAD. C'mere, you.

(The DADS kiss again.)

MOURNERS.

'CAUSE NOW WE LOVE, LOVE, LOVE!
WE LOVE YOUR DEAD…

BOTH DADS.	MOURNERS.
THEY'RE UP THERE DISCO DANCING	OO…
TO THE THUMP OF ANGEL WINGS.	
	YEAH!

BOTH DADS.   **MOURNERS.**

 THEY GRAB A MATE   OO...
 AND ROLLER SKATE!
 WHILE JUDY GARLAND
  SINGS!

        YEAH!
 THEY LIVE A PLAYFUL   OO...
  AFTERLIFE
 THAT'S FANCY-FREE AND   OO,
  RECKLESS!

KURT'S DAD.   YEAH!

 THEY SWING UPON THE
  PEARLY GATES –

ALL.

 AND WEAR A PEARLY NECKLACE!

        MOURNERS.

BOTH DADS.   WHOO!

 THEY WERE NOT DIRTY!

        NO!
 THEY WERE GOOD MEN!   THEY WERE GOOD MEN!
        WHOA!
 AND NOW THEY'RE HAPPY   AND NOW THEY'RE HAPPY
  BEAR CUBS   BEAR CUBS
 IN THE LORD'S BIG DEN!   IN THE LORD'S BIG DEN!
 GO FORTH AND LOVE EACH
  OTHER NOW,
 LIKE OUR BOYS WOULD
  HAVE DONE.

BOTH DADS & ALTO/TENOR
 MOURNERS.   **SOPRANO/BASS MOURNERS.**

 WE'LL TEACH THE WORLD   WE'LL TEACH THE WORLD
  TO LOVE...   TO LOVE...
        THE WORLD TO LOVE...
 THE WORLD TO LOVE...   WORLD TO LOVE...

BOTH DADS.

 I LOVE MY DEAD GAY SON!   NOT HALF BAD,
 MY SON!   YOUR DEAD GAY SON!
        WISH I HAD

MY SON!   YOUR DEAD GAY SON!
                                 THANK YOU, DAD,
                                 FOR YOUR
DEAD GAY SON!   DEAD GAY SON!

[MUSIC NO. 11A "MY DEAD GAY SON PLAYOFF"]

Scene Two

(**J.D.** *and* **VERONICA** *cross the stage, back at school. They are alone.*)

J.D. Well, what is that I smell in the air? Tolerance? Inclusion? Love? How often can you say it's a good day to live in Sherwood, Ohio? You're welcome, town.

VERONICA. You don't have to be so smug about it.

J.D. Your love keeps me humble.

(*He again tries to kiss her cheek. This time she allows it.*)

So who's next? Heather Duke?

VERONICA. What?

J.D. She started that rumor about you. We could underline meaningful passages in her copy of *Moby Dick* if you know what I mean.

(**DEAD KURT,** **DEAD RAM,** *and* **DEAD CHANDLER** *appear in a scary tableau. The* **JOCKS** *are in the underpants they were wearing when they died, no visible gunshot wounds. Again, only* **VERONICA** *sees them.*)

VERONICA. No!

(*Lights black out on the* **DEAD TEENS.** **VERONICA,** *badly shaken, turns attention back to* **J.D.***)*

Three people are dead. This ends here.

J.D. Or what?

VERONICA. …Or I'm breaking up with you.

J.D. Any war has casualties. Doesn't mean it's not worth fighting. But what, you'd rather go to jail? And give a free pass to the cannibals? The assholes who make the world so unbearable, you can't stand to go on living?

(**VERONICA** *studies him.*)

VERONICA. J.D., how did your mother die?

J.D. You really want to know?

VERONICA. I do.

J.D. My father said it was an accident, but she knew what she was doing. I was nine. My father got hired to blow up this condemned library in Texas. Norwegian in the boiler room, the usual. But this day, my mom drives out to the demolition site, me in the back seat, reading a comic book. She gets out of the car and walks into the building two minutes before Dad blew it up. She waved at me out the window, and then…

(With a graceful hand gesture.) …Kabooooom. She left me.

VERONICA. I'm really sorry.

J.D. It's okay. The pain gives me clarity. You and I are special. We have a lot of work to do.

VERONICA. What work?

J.D. Making the world a decent place for people who are decent.

VERONICA. And when does it end?

J.D. When every asshole is dead.

(VERONICA shoves him hard. He stumbles and falls to the floor. He stays there, shocked into silence under the following.)

VERONICA. Aaagh!

[MUSIC NO. 12 "SEVENTEEN"]

FINE! WE'RE DAMAGED.
REALLY DAMAGED.
BUT THAT DOES NOT MAKE US WISE!
WE'RE NOT SPECIAL.
WE'RE NOT DIFFERENT.
WE DON'T CHOOSE WHO LIVES OR DIES.

LET'S BE NORMAL.
SEE BAD MOVIES.
SNEAK A BEER AND WATCH TV.
WE'LL BAKE BROWNIES.
WE'LL GO BOWLING.
DON'T YOU WANT A LIFE WITH ME?

CAN'T WE BE SEVENTEEN?
THAT'S ALL I WANT TO DO.

VERONICA.

> IF YOU COULD LET ME IN,
> I COULD BE GOOD WITH YOU.

VERONICA.

> PEOPLE HURT US –   **J.D.**
>
>   OR THEY VANISH –
>
> AND YOU'RE RIGHT,
> THAT REALLY BLOWS.
> BUT WE LET GO.
>
>   TAKE A DEEP BREATH.
>
> THEN GO BUY SOME
>   SUMMER CLOTHES.

VERONICA.

> WE'LL GO CAMPING.   **J.D.**
>
>   PLAY SOME POKER.
>
> AND WE'LL EAT SOME
>   CHILI FRIES.
> MAYBE PROM NIGHT.
>
>   MAYBE DANCING.
>
> DON'T STOP LOOKING
> IN MY EYES.   YOUR EYES.

*(***VERONICA*** offers* **J.D.** *her hand. He now looks* **VERONICA** *in the eyes for the first time. He stands and crosses to her.)*

VERONICA & J.D.

> CAN'T WE BE SEVENTEEN?
> IS THAT SO HARD TO DO?
> IF YOU COULD LET ME IN,
> I COULD BE GOOD WITH YOU.
> LET US BE SEVENTEEN,
> IF WE'VE STILL GOT THE RIGHT.

VERONICA.

> SO, WHAT'S IT GONNA BE?
> I WANNA BE WITH YOU.   **J.D.**
>
>   I WANNA
> WANNA BE WITH YOU   BE WITH YOU…
> TONIGHT!   …TONIGHT!

(They embrace.)

YEAH, WE'RE DAMAGED.

BUT YOUR LOVE'S TOO
   GOOD TO LOSE.
HOLD ME TIGHTER.

I'LL STAY IF I'M WHAT YOU
   CHOOSE.

IF I AM WHAT YOU
   CHOOSE...

'CAUSE YOU'RE THE ONE I
   CHOOSE.

YOU'RE THE ONE I
   CHOOSE.

(They kiss.)

BADLY DAMAGED.
BUT YOUR LOVE'S TOO
   GOOD TO LOSE.

EVEN CLOSER.

CAN'T WE BE SEVENTEEN...

IF WE'VE STILL GOT THE
   RIGHT...

YOU'RE THE ONE I
   CHOOSE.
YOU'RE THE ONE I
   CHOOSE.

Scene Three

(They part, and **J.D.** *exits. The school bell rings.)*

[MUSIC NO. 12A "HAPPILY EVER AFTER"]

*(***DEAD CHANDLER** *steps up behind* **VERONICA**.)*

DEAD CHANDLER. And they lived happily ever after.

*(***VERONICA** *jumps, startled.)*

You really believe that? You think it all goes back to normal? Oh, don't give me that wounded look. You know exactly what he is. And you love it.

VERONICA. Just stop talking.

DEAD CHANDLER. Only a *true* dead best friend will give it to you straight.

*(***MS. FLEMING** *enters, holding an armful of costumes.)*

MS. FLEMING. Veronica! The special assembly starts in ten minutes. Why aren't you backstage? We are saving lives here!

DEAD CHANDLER. I wouldn't trust her to save coupons.

(She follows **VERONICA** *as the lights change.)*

(We're now on the high school stage preparing for a school assembly. A hand-painted banner reads "ROTTWEILERS TAKE A BITE OUT OF SUICIDE!")

(Students mill about, making preparations. Among them are **DUKE**, **MCNAMARA**, *and* **MARTHA**. **DUKE** *is wearing Chandler red.)*

MS. FLEMING. Pedal to the metal, kids. Show a little hustle.

(She hands out jackets to the **STUDENTS**.*)*

(Out to house, pointing.) Denise, tell the news crews they can set up the cameras, there, there and there.

(To a group of **STUDENTS**.*)* Okay, let's review your hand choreography, precision is key.

*(***DUKE** *and* **MCNAMARA** *slip into their Glee Club jackets.)*

MCNAMARA. I'm kinda looking forward to being on TV.

DUKE. Did you have a brain tumor for breakfast?

MCNAMARA. No, I had oatmeal.

DUKE. Ugh.

(MARTHA hurries up to VERONICA.)

MARTHA. Veronica. Can I talk to you? In private?

VERONICA. Sure, what?

MARTHA. Something doesn't add up. I think Ram and Kurt were murdered.

(All action freezes except for MARTHA, VERONICA, and DEAD CHANDLER. DEAD CHANDLER is gleefully malicious.)

DEAD CHANDLER. Well, fuck me gently with a chainsaw!

(VERONICA yanks MARTHA out of earshot of the other STUDENTS, who resume silent motion.)

Nancy Drew is on to you, Veronica.

VERONICA. Why would you say that? They found a suicide note.

MARTHA. It could have been faked. I mean, *you* forge stuff all the time right?

DEAD CHANDLER. I am in love with this fat girl!

VERONICA. Who'd want to kill Ram and Kurt?

MARTHA. I'm thinking your friend J.D. Remember the way he went after them in the lunchroom?

(DEAD RAM and DEAD KURT enter.)

DEAD KURT. Right, right, that's like motive and shit!

DEAD RAM. Veronica's going to lady prison!

MARTHA. I want to look in J.D.'s locker. I thought maybe you could get me the combination.

DEAD CHANDLER. I bet there's all kinds of interesting things in that locker.

Maybe some *ich luge* bullets?

(VERONICA tries to ignore DEAD CHANDLER.)

VERONICA. Martha…this is a pretty wild theory.

MARTHA. I don't care what they were saying at the funeral.

(The following dialogue overlaps.)

Ram was not gay.

DEAD KURT. Awwww…

DEAD RAM. Shut up, Kurt.

MARTHA. He kissed me, remember? On the kickball field.

VERONICA. Yeah, in kindergarten!

DEAD KURT. Oh gross, I remember that!

DEAD RAM. Shut up, Kurt.

MARTHA. My heart knows the truth.

DEAD KURT. You should totally get up in that!

DEAD RAM. Shut up!

MARTHA. Why would Ram write me that note if he didn't still feel something?

DEAD KURT. She ain't 'fraid of no ghost!

DEAD RAM. Aaagh!

MARTHA. Why would he invite me to his homecoming party?

(Overlapping dialogue ends.)

DEAD CHANDLER. You want to stop her? You know what to say.

MARTHA. I'm gonna confront J.D.

*(She turns to leave. **VERONICA** emits a cruel laugh, which prompts **MARTHA** to turn back, unnerved.)*

VERONICA. You floor me, Martha. You really do.

MARTHA. What do you mean?

VERONICA. Ram didn't write that love note. *I* did.

MARTHA. No.

VERONICA. Yeah, the Heathers put me up to it. The whole school was in on the joke. And nobody laughed harder than Ram. He didn't love you. He was a dick, he's dead, move on!

(**MARTHA** *stares for a beat. She then turns and walks away.*)

Shit.

(**VERONICA**, *distraught, turns to* **DEAD CHANDLER**.)

I had to hurt her. You see that, right? If J.D. ever caught her snooping around his stuff, he'd…

DEAD CHANDLER. …Kill her? Is that what you're afraid of?

VERONICA. I…

DEAD CHANDLER. That's what I thought. C'mon, assholes.

(*She snaps her fingers, and* **DEAD KURT** *and* **DEAD RAM** *follow.*)

(*As the* **DEAD TEENS** *exit,* **VERONICA** *glances at* **J.D.**, *who stands, perhaps on an upper level, tinkering with a spotlight. He's working with the A.V. Club, handling tech for the upcoming presentation. He sees* **VERONICA** *looking at him. He smiles and nods at her.*)

VERONICA. Dear diary. What am I doing?

[MUSIC NO. 12B "PLACES FOR ASSEMBLY"]

(**MS. FLEMING** *hands* **MARTHA** *a jacket. She refuses it.*)

MARTHA. I'm sorry, I can't be in this assembly.

MS. FLEMING. (*Rising panic.*) What? No, you're my second soprano. If you're not in position it will completely unbalance the stage picture.

MARTHA. I'm having a bad day. Emotionally. Veronica said that –

MS. FLEMING. You're a little sad. I get that. But remember how much your support means to all your classmates who worked hard to help get this very important message out to the world.

(*She helps* **MARTHA** *back on with her jacket.*)

And if that doesn't put a smile on your face, think about how participation in this assembly counts for one third of your grade! Feeling better?

MARTHA. Um…

MS. FLEMING. Good talk!

(The assembly is about to begin. **MS. FLEMING** *takes center stage. The* **STUDENTS** *assemble behind her, including* **MARTHA**. **MARTHA** *turns her back on* **VERONICA**.*)*

Okay, big smiles everybody. Lights please!

(J.D. *turns on his spotlight as the lights change.)*

[MUSIC NO. 13 "SHINE A LIGHT"]

Hello Westerberg!

(Works crowd as needed, ad-libbing freely.) Welcome to our special assembly. I want you to ignore the television cameras and the news crew. They're just here to document this significant moment: whether to kill yourself or not is one of the most important decisions a teenager can make. So you know what I'm gonna do right now?

HIPSTER DORK. *(Calls out.)* Kill yourself on stage?

MS. FLEMING. That's not productive, Dwight.

(To audience.) My senior thesis at Berkeley was on the subject of pediatric psychotherapeutic musicology. So I speak with some authority when I tell you that the way to eliminate suicide is by first eliminating fear. By creating a safe zone in which we are all equal!

DEEP INSIDE OF EV'RYONE
THERE'S A HOT BALL OF SHAME.
GUILT, REGRETS, ANXIETY;
FEARS WE DARE NOT NAME.
BUT IF WE SHOW THE UGLY PARTS
THAT WE HIDE AWAY,
THEY TURN OUT TO BE BEAUTIFUL
BY THE LIGHT OF DAY!

MS. FLEMING.

WHY NOT	**STUDENTS.**
SHINE, SHINE, SHINE A LIGHT	SHINE, SHINE, SHINE A LIGHT
ON YOUR DEEPEST FEAR.	

LET IN SUNLIGHT
AND YOUR PAIN WILL
    DISAPPEAR!
SHINE, SHINE, SHI-INE,
AND YOUR SCARS AND YOUR
    FLAWS
WILL LOOK LOVELY
    BECAUSE YOU SHINE...
YOU SHINE A LIGHT.

LET IN SUNLIGHT NOW,

SHINE, SHINE, SHI-INE,
OO, OO!

WILL LOOK LOVELY
    BECAUSE YOU SHINE...

SHINE, SHINE, SHINE, A
    LIGHT!

OO HOO.

STONER CHICK.
    EV'RY DAY'S A BATTLEFIELD
    WHEN PRIDE'S ON THE LINE.

PREPPY STUD.
    I ATTACK YOUR WEAKNESSES,

MS. FLEMING, STONER & PREPPY.
    AND PRAY YOU DON'T SEE
    MINE.

BELEAGUERED GEEK.
    BUT IF I SHARE MY UGLY
    PARTS,

**MS. FLEMING, GEEK & NEW WAVE
GIRL.**
    AND YOU SHOW ME YOURS,

GEEK & NEW WAVE.
    OUR LOVE CAN KNOCK OUR
    WALLS DOWN,

**MS. FLEMING, STONER, PREPPY,
GEEK & NEW WAVE.**
    AND UNLOCK ALL OUR
    DOORS!

MS. FLEMING.
    SHINE, SHINE, SHINE A
    LIGHT,
    ON YOUR DEEPEST FEAR!

SHINE, SHINE, SHINE, A
    LIGHT!
OO... OO...

OO...

OO...

OO...

OO...

OH...

AH, AH, AH, AH!
SHINE, SHINE, SHINE A
    LIGHT!

STUDENTS.

MS. FLEMING.   LET IN SUNLIGHT NOW!

AND YOUR PAIN WILL
    DISAPPEAR!   DISAPPEAR!

MS. FLEMING.

WHO WANTS TO SHARE WHAT'S IN THEIR HEART?
NO VOLUNTEERS? FINE, I'LL START.
MY NAME'S PAULINE. I LIVE ALONE.
MY HUSBAND LEFT. MY KIDS ARE GROWN.
IN THE SIXTIES, LOVE WAS FREE;
THAT DID NOT WORK OUT WELL FOR ME.
THE REVOLUTION CAME AND WENT;
TRIED TO CHANGE THE WORLD, BARELY MADE A DENT.
I HAVE STRUGGLED WITH DESPAIR.
I JOINED A CULT, CHOPPED OFF MY HAIR,
I CHANT, I PRAY, BUT GOD'S NOT THERE.
(To someone in the audience.) SO STEVE, I'M ENDING OUR
    AFFAIR!

*(She picks on some poor sap in the audience who thought
it was cool to get a front-row seat. She should feel free to
mess with him, saying things like, "Stand up." "Take off
your glasses." "Is that your wife?" "Sit down." "Let me
touch the beard one last time." Once she's done, she says:)*

…And I faked it. Every single time.
(Deep, cleansing breath.) That felt fan-frickin'-TAStic!
One! Two! Take me home, kids!

STUDENTS.
SHINE, SHINE, SHINE A
MS. FLEMING.   LIGHT!
ON YOUR DEEPEST FEAR!

                                     LET IN SUNLIGHT NOW!

AND YOUR PAIN WILL
    DISAPPEAR!

                                     SHINE, SHINE, SHINE,
AND YOUR SCARS AND   OO, OO!
    YOUR FLAWS
WILL LOOK LOVELY   WILL LOOK LOVELY
    BECAUSE YOU SHINE!   BECAUSE YOU SHINE!

YOU SHINE...   AH...
YOU SHINE A LIGHT!

                                  SHINE, SHINE, SHINE A
                                      LIGHT!
                                  SHINE, SHINE, SHINE A
                                      LIGHT!
                                  SHINE, SHINE, SHINE A
                                      LIGHT!
                                  SHINE, SHINE, SHINE A
                                      LIGHT!
SHINE, SHINE A LIGHT!   SHINE, SHINE, SHINE A
                                      LIGHT!
SHINE, SHINE A LIGHT!   SHINE, SHINE, SHINE A
                                      LIGHT!
SHINE, SHINE A LIGHT!   SHINE, SHINE, SHINE A
                                      LIGHT!
SHINE A LIGHT! YEAH!   SHINE A LIGHT! YEAH!

[MUSIC NO. 13A "SHINE A LIGHT PLAYOFF"]

MS. FLEMING. C'mon, kids! Work with me! I want you to grab hold of your fear and drag it out into the light where everyone can look at it! Anyone?

(MARTHA raises her hand, tentative. MS. FLEMING, looking out to the audience, doesn't see her.)

Anyone at all...

(As she turns back from the audience, MCNAMARA raises her hand.)

MCNAMARA. I've thought about killing myself!

(MARTHA glumly lowers her hand as MS. FLEMING recognizes MCNAMARA.)

MS. FLEMING. Heather McNamara, share that pain!

(VERONICA steps forward.)

VERONICA. Heather, don't do this. Not here

(MCNAMARA hesitates, aware everyone is looking at her.)

MS. FLEMING. No, no, no. Don't stop, Heather.

VERONICA.	MS. FLEMING.
Let's go somewhere and talk. Just you and me.	Veronica Sawyer, no one gave you permission to speak.

MS. FLEMING. You're in a safe place, Heather. Just you and me and the classmates who love you. Share. It's gonna be okay.

[MUSIC NO. 14 "LIFEBOAT"]

MCNAMARA. The guy I used to date killed himself because he was gay for his linebacker. And my best friend seemed to have it all together, but now she's gone too. Now my stomach's hurting worse and worse, and every morning on the bus I feel my heart beating louder and faster, and I'm like, "Jesus, I'm on the frickin' bus again 'cause all my rides to school are dead."

(Lights have converged on **MCNAMARA.** *The room is eerie and still.)*

I FLOAT IN A BOAT
ON A RAGING BLACK OCEAN.
LOW IN THE WATER
AND NOWHERE TO GO.
THE TINIEST LIFEBOAT,
WITH PEOPLE I KNOW.
COLD, CLAMMY AND CROWDED.
THE PEOPLE SMELL DESP'RATE.
WE'LL SINK ANY MINUTE,
SO SOMEONE MUST GO.
THE TINIEST LIFEBOAT,
WITH PEOPLE I KNOW.

EV'RYONE'S PUSHING,
EV'RYONE'S FIGHTING,
STORMS ARE APPROACHING,
THERE'S NOWHERE TO HIDE!

IF I SAY THE WRONG THING
OR I WEAR THE WRONG OUTFIT
THEY'LL THROW ME RIGHT OVER THE SIDE!

I'M HUGGING MY KNEES,
AND THE CAPTAIN IS POINTING.
WELL, WHO MADE *HER* CAPTAIN?
STILL, THE WEAKEST MUST GO.
THE TINIEST LIFEBOAT,
FULL OF PEOPLE I KNOW.
THE TINIEST LIFEBOAT,
FULL OF PEOPLE I KNOW.

(She ends the song facing downstage, soul bared to the audience.)

(The lights return to normal. Everyone else watches in stunned silence.)

(Dawning horror registers on **MCNAMARA**'s *face as she realizes she has just said all of this out loud. She can feel everyone staring at her.)*

*(***DUKE*** *is the first to recover and speak.)*

DUKE. What's your damage, Heather?

[MUSIC NO. 14A "SHINE A LIGHT (REPRISE)"]

Are you saying Westerberg's not a nice place?

MS. FLEMING. Heather!

DUKE.

Where's your school spirit?	**MS. FLEMING.**
You don't deserve to wear	This is not the way we
Westerberg colors! Why	behave at Westerberg.
don't you hop in your little	That's enough, Heather.
lifeboat and catch a gnarly	Cameras. Heather, shut
wave over to Remington!	your cake-hole!

(Gathered **STUDENTS** *laugh.* **MS. FLEMING** *struggles to maintain control.)*

MS. FLEMING. Knock it off!

(To the **GROUP**.*)* All right people, settle down!

STONER. Aw, look…Heather's gonna cry!

DUKE. God, what a baby!

*(***MCNAMARA*** *runs for the exit, devastated.* **MS. FLEMING** *whirls on* **DUKE**, *furious.)*

MS. FLEMING. That's it, young lady – one month's detention! *(Out to house.)* Turn off the cameras! Turn them off, god dammit!

VERONICA. Is that all you care about? TV cameras?

MS. FLEMING. I care about saving lives. Heather Duke ruined a valuable teaching moment –

VERONICA. – Valuable?! None of us want this spectacle. To be experimented on like guinea pigs, patronized like bunny rabbits!

MS. FLEMING. I don't patronize bunny rabbits!

*(**DEAD CHANDLER** steps up to **VERONICA**, unseen by the others.)*

DEAD CHANDLER. This is their big secret. The adults are powerless.

VERONICA. Heather trusted you! You said you'd protect her!

DEAD CHANDLER. They can't help us. Nobody can help us.

VERONICA. You're useless!

DEAD CHANDLER. We're alone in the ocean!

*(Impulsively, **VERONICA** yells at her fellow **STUDENTS**.)*

VERONICA. You're all idiots! Heather Chandler was a bully, just like Kurt and Ram! They didn't kill themselves! I killed them!

*(Stunned silence. **VERONICA** looks up at **J.D.** – he is staring at her in mute horror.)*

*(Suddenly, **DUKE** breaks the tension by laughing. The **STUDENTS** quickly join in, relieved.)*

DUKE. God! Some people will say anything if they think it'll make them popular. You're worse than McNamara.

VERONICA. *(Remembering.)* Heather. Heather!

(She runs out.)

*(Lights up on the girls' bathroom. **MCNAMARA** enters, struggling to open a prescription bottle.)*

MCNAMARA. Stupid childproof caps!

(She gasps in horror as **IMAGINARY STUDENTS** *surround her, led by* **IMAGINARY DUKE.** *The* **IMAGINARY STUDENTS** *all wear 3D glasses.)*

IMAGINARY DUKE.

AW, LOOK!

HEATHER'S GOING TO –	**IMAGINARY STUDENTS.**
WHINE, WHINE, WHINE ALL NIGHT!	WHINE, WHINE, WHINE ALL NIGHT!

*(***IMAGINARY DUKE** *grabs the pill bottle from* **MCNAMARA** *and opens it.)*

YOU DON'T DESERVE TO LIVE.

WHY NOT KILL YOURSELF?	WHY NOT KILL YOURSELF?

*(***IMAGINARY DUKE** *hands the open pill bottle back to* **MCNAMARA.** *)*

HERE, HAVE A SEDATIVE.

WHINE, WHINE, WHI-INE!	WHINE, WHINE, WHI-INE!
LIKE THERE'S	
NO SANTA CLAUS.	BOO HOO.
YOU'RE PATHETIC	YOU'RE PATHETIC
BECAUSE YOU WHINE...	BECAUSE YOU WHINE...
YOU WHINE ALL NIGHT!	
YOUR ASS IS OFF THE TEAM.	WHINE.
DEEP DOWN, YOU'VE ALWAYS KNOWN –	WHINE.
YOU DON'T DESERVE THE DREAM.	WHINE.
YOU'RE GONNA DIE ALONE!	WHINE.
DIE ALONE! DIE ALONE!	DIE ALONE! DIE ALONE!
DIE ALONE! DIE ALONE!	DIE ALONE! DIE ALONE!

(Song ends. **IMAGINARY DUKE** *and the* **IMAGINARY STUDENTS** *exit as* **MCNAMARA** *stuffs pills in her mouth. Lights change as* **VERONICA** *enters the bathroom.)*

*(***VERONICA** *sees* **MCNAMARA** *with her cheeks full of pills.)*

VERONICA. Heather, no!

(She knocks the pills out of **MCNAMARA**'s *mouth, sending* **MCNAMARA** *sinking to her knees, coughing.)*

MCNAMARA. Suicide is a private thing!

VERONICA. Throwing your life away so *USA Today* can print your picture under the headline "troubled teens" – that's the least private thing I can think of.

MCNAMARA. But what about Heather and Ram and Kurt?

VERONICA. If everyone jumped off a bridge, young lady, would you?

MCNAMARA. Probably.

[MUSIC NO. 14B "YOU'RE WELCOME, MCNAMARA"]

VERONICA. Oh. Well, if you were happy all the time, you wouldn't be human. You'd be a game show host.

MCNAMARA. Thanks for coming after me.

VERONICA. You're welcome.

*(***MCNAMARA*** embraces* **VERONICA**. *Lights change…)*

Scene Four

(J.D.'s living room. **J.D.** *paces.* **VERONICA** *enters.)*

VERONICA. So I'm guessing you're mad about that confession, huh?

J.D. Not mad. Confused. You wanted us to be normal teenagers. I did that. I joined the goddamn A.V. Club – for you!

VERONICA. I know.

J.D. Do you know what would have happened if they'd actually believed your confession? Handcuffs. Separate cells. Cops trying to turn us against each other. Right before they ship us off to different prisons. Is that what you want? Be honest.

VERONICA. Of course not.

J.D. Well, what then?

VERONICA. Everyone's cashing in on these fake suicides, making it about them. It's a sick trend and we started it.

J.D. Turning ourselves in won't stop human nature.

VERONICA. Then *what?* Fleming's little kumbaya party almost ended with Heather Mac dead on a bathroom floor.

J.D. Fleming's not the problem. Heather Duke is. She's the one who made McNamara want to die. If you want to slay the dragon, cut off its head.

VERONICA. Stop.

J.D. But no, you'd rather treat bubonic plague with Band-Aids. We had the power to change things. But we gave that up to be "normal teenagers."
(Mock-waving in the distance.) Good luck at school tomorrow, Heather Mac, hope you don't die!

VERONICA. We are out of the change business.

J.D.	**VERONICA.**
If you want to give it all up and let the world slide into the trash, fine! But don't act surprised when we all smell a little like garbage!	You made me a promise, remember? I'm holding you to it! Are you even listening? Stop talking over me!

VERONICA. *(Emphatic.)* You promised!

J.D. *(Beat, softening.)* All right. I'm sorry.

(**BIG BUD DEAN** *enters, intense.*)

BIG BUD. Stop playing grab-ass and wait for me in the car.

J.D. I'm in the middle of something.

BIG BUD. I need backup. Our friends have another job for us.

(Same gentle hand gesture **J.D.** *used.)* Kabooooooom.

J.D. I said I'm busy.

(**BIG BUD** *stops, turns, and puts an arm around* **J.D.**)

BIG BUD. Lotta pretty women out there, sport. I can make another son any time I want. Now get your ass in that car.

(He releases **J.D.** *and exits.* **J.D.** *steams a moment, pulls out a pistol, and points it in the direction of his father. At the last minute, he turns and shoots the TV, which explodes in sparks.)*

BIG BUD. *(Offstage.)* Dammit, Jason, no firearms in the house!

(**J.D.** *sees the horrified look on* **VERONICA**'s *face.)*

J.D. What? It pissed off my dad. It's funny.

VERONICA. None of this is funny! Why are you carrying a loaded weapon?

J.D. Protection.

VERONICA. From what? Re-runs?

(**J.D.** *takes a breath and smiles, composing himself, his charming and persuasive mask back in place.)*

J.D. We gotta stop pretending. This is who I am. If you don't like it, take it up with him.
(Points in the direction **BIG BUD** *exited.)* He made me.

[MUSIC NO. 15 "I SAY NO"]

VERONICA. *(Horrified.)* Ohh. Martha was right about you.

J.D. Now let's have a real conversation.

VERONICA. She was right and I broke her heart.

J.D. Let's talk about Heather Duke.

VERONICA. No, let's talk about you!

> *(Lights change.* **J.D.** *freezes. Time has stopped for* **VERONICA.** *)*

VERONICA.

> YOU ARE A DRUG.
> YOU ARE A POISON PILL.
> I'VE GOT TO KICK THIS HABIT NOW
> OR ELSE I NEVER WILL.
> I LOVED THE RUSH
> WHEN YOU WOULD HOLD ME CLOSE.
> BUT YOU WILL NOT BE SATISFIED UNTIL I OVERDOSE.
> THIS IS IT!
> HIT THE BRAKE.
> I AM FIN'LLY AWAKE.
> LET ME BE
> LET ME GO.
> YOU NEED HELP I CAN'T PROVIDE.
> I AM NOT QUALIFIED.
> THIS TROUBLED TEEN
> IS GETTING CLEAN.
> I SAY NO.

> *(Lights change.* **J.D.** *unfreezes and steps forward, smiling.)*

J.D.	**VERONICA.**
Veronica, who else is gonna –	NO! NO!
	NO! NO!

VERONICA.

> DON'T SAY A WORD.
> YOU SPEAK AND I CAVE IN.
> YOU'LL TWIST THE TRUTH AGAIN
> AND DRILL DEEP DOWN BENEATH MY SKIN.
> YOU SAID YOU'D CHANGE –
> AND I BELIEVED IN YOU.
> BUT YOU'RE STILL USING ME
> TO JUSTIFY THE HARM YOU DO.

VERONICA.

THIS IS IT!	**ENSEMBLE.**
HIT THE BRAKE.	OH.
CALL IT ALL MY MISTAKE,	
LONG AS YOU	OH.
LET ME GO.	
YOU NEED HELP I CAN'T	OH.
PROVIDE.	
I'M NOT BONNIE, YOU'RE	
NOT CLYDE.	
IT'S NOT TOO LATE,	OH.
I'M GETTING STRAIGHT.	
I SAY NO!	WHOA! WHOA!

(J.D. is starting to get worried. He steps toward VERONICA, but she's determined to evade him.)

VERONICA.

BLAME YOUR CHILDHOOD, BLAME YOUR DAD –
BLAME THE LIFE YOU NEVER HAD.
BUT HURTING PEOPLE? THAT'S YOUR CHOICE, MY FRIEND.
'CAUSE I BELIEVE THAT LOVE WILL WIN
AND HATE WILL EARN YOU NOTHING IN THE END –
THIS IS THE END!

J.D. But I love you!

(VERONICA flinches. J.D.'s hand has raised, accidentally pointing the gun at her.)

VERONICA. Dude.

(Realizing his error, J.D. quickly lowers the gun, but it's too late. The damage is irreversible.)

VERONICA.

THIS IS IT!	**ENSEMBLE.**
I WON'T CRY.	OH!
STARTING NOW I WILL TRY	OH!
TO PAY BACK ALL THE	OH!
KARMA I OWE.	
START AGAIN, SOMEWHERE	START AGAIN, SOMEWHERE
NEW.	NEW.

FAR FROM COOL GUYS LIKE YOU.	FAR FROM COOL GUYS LIKE YOU.
SO GOODBYE, 'CAUSE NOW I –	OH... OH...
I SAY NO.	WHOA!
JUST IN TIME, I SAY NO.	WHOA! WHOA!
SOMEHOW I'M SAYING NO.	WHOA! WHOA!
JUST SAY NO.	WHOA!
I SAY NO!	WHOA!
NO!	

(VERONICA *exits, leaving* **J.D.** *alone with his gun. He stands motionless as we hear offstage stomping and clapping...*)

Scene Five

[MUSIC NO. 15A "HEY YO WESTERBERG"]

*(**MCNAMARA** enters, leading some **STUDENTS** across stage, working them up for the upcoming pep rally.)*

*(**MARTHA** stands, watching the cheerleaders pass her by, ignored.)*

MCNAMARA & STUDENTS.
WHOA...OA!

MCNAMARA. Who's ready for the big game?

MCNAMARA & STUDENTS.
WHOA...OA!

MCNAMARA. Let's get psyched!

*(**J.D.** tucks the gun into the back of his pants, still staring offstage where **VERONICA** exited. He seems unaware of the crowd gathering.)*

*(**MCNAMARA** leads a cheer.)*

MCNAMARA & STUDENTS.
HEY YO WESTERBERG!
TELL ME WHAT'S THAT SOUND?
HERE COMES WESTERBERG,
COMING TO PUT YOU IN THE GROUND!
GO GO WESTERBERG,
GIVE A GREAT BIG YELL!
WESTERBERG WILL KNOCK YOU OUT
AND SEND YOU STRAIGHT TO HELL!

*(**MARTHA** watches **J.D.** for a beat. He looks up, feeling her gaze. He shrugs and exits – she's beneath his notice.)*

*(**MARTHA** is jostled by a couple of the cheering **STUDENTS**. Nobody bothers to speak to her or excuse themselves.)*

*(**MARTHA** exits as **MCNAMARA** leads the other **STUDENTS** offstage.)*

*(Lights change. **J.D.** approaches **DUKE** and hands her an envelope)*

J.D. I now know thee, thou clear spirit.

DUKE. That's from *Moby Dick*.

J.D. I appreciate a well-read woman.

(DUKE opens the envelope.)

DUKE. What's in the envelope?

(She gasps in horror as she rifles through the photos inside.)

Oh shit!

J.D. Just a reminder that at one time, around age six I'm guessing, you and Martha Dunnstock were friends.

(Lights up on MARTHA, standing alone, perhaps on an upper level of the stage, lost in thought.)

DUKE. Where did you get these? Did Veronica give them to you?

(J.D. takes back the photos.)

What do you want? Money?

J.D. A favor.

DUKE. No way.

J.D. I love this one of you and Martha in the bathtub together.

DUKE. *(False bravado.)* Those photos are ancient history. Nobody cares about the past.

(Lights dim on J.D. and DUKE and brighten on MARTHA.)

Nobody cares about Martha Dumptruck.

(MARTHA removes her glasses and pockets them. Her location remains unclear.)

[MUSIC NO. 16 "KINDERGARTEN BOYFRIEND"]

MARTHA.
THERE WAS A BOY I MET IN KINDERGARTEN.
HE WAS SWEET, HE SAID THAT I WAS SMART.
HE WAS GOOD AT SPORTS AND PEOPLE LIKED HIM.
AND AT NAPTIME, ONCE, WE SHARED A MAT.
I DIDN'T SLEEP, I SAT AND WATCHED HIM BREATHING;

MARTHA.

WATCHED HIM DREAM FOR NEARLY HALF AN HOUR.
OO... THEN HE WOKE UP.

HE PULLED A SCAB OFF, ONE TIME, PLAYING KICKBALL.
KISSED ME QUICK, THEN PRESSED IT IN MY HAND.
I TOOK THAT SCAB AND PUT IT IN A LOCKET.
ALL YEAR LONG I WORE IT NEAR MY HEART.
HE DIDN'T CARE IF I WAS THIN OR PRETTY,
AND HE WAS MINE UNTIL WE HIT FIRST GRADE.
OO... THEN HE WOKE UP.

LAST NIGHT I DREAMED
A HORSE WITH WINGS
FLEW DOWN INTO MY HOMEROOM.
ON ITS BACK THERE HE SAT,
AND HE HELD OUT HIS ARMS.
SO WE SAILED ABOVE THE GYM,
ACROSS THE FACULTY PARKING LOT.
MY KINDERGARTEN BOYFRIEND AND I...
AND A HORSE WITH WINGS.

NOW WE'RE ALL GROWN UP AND WE KNOW BETTER.
NOW WE RECOGNIZE THE WAY THINGS ARE.
CERTAIN BOYS ARE JUST FOR KINDERGARTEN,
CERTAIN GIRLS ARE MEANT TO BE ALONE.

(Lights change to reveal **MARTHA** *is standing on the edge of a bridge.)*

BUT I BELIEVE THAT ANY DREAM WORTH HAVING
IS A DREAM THAT SHOULD NOT HAVE TO END.
SO I'LL BUILD A DREAM THAT I CAN LIVE IN,
AND THIS TIME I'M NEVER WAKING UP.

AND WE'LL SOAR
ABOVE THE TREES,
OVER CARS AND CROQUET LAWNS.
PAST THE CHURCH,
AND THE LAKE,
AND THE TRI-COUNTY MALL!
WE WILL FLY
THROUGH THE DAWN,

TO A NEW KINDERGARTEN...
WHERE NAPTIME IS CENTURIES LONG.
OO... OO... OO... OO...
OO OO.

(She raises her arms, as if to fly. As she leans back...)

(Blackout.)

[MUSIC NO. 16A "TRANSITION TO PETITION"]

Scene Six

(School lunchroom. A worried **VERONICA** *sits with* **MCNAMARA**.*)*

VERONICA. Martha wasn't in homeroom today.

MCNAMARA. Well, did you try calling her house?

VERONICA. It just goes straight to her answering machine. Where the hell could she be?

*(***DUKE** *enters with a clipboard.)*

DUKE. Hey guys! Missed you after third period.

VERONICA. We were avoiding you because you're a terrible person.

DUKE. Fine, skip the foreplay. Sign this.

(She offers the clipboard to **MCNAMARA**, *who hesitates.* **DUKE** *is insistent.* **MCNAMARA** *sighs, takes the clipboard, and signs.)*

VERONICA. What is this?

DUKE. It's a petition to have MTV throw a spring break blowout to help raise suicide awareness. I got everybody to sign. People love me. I'm gonna make an inspirational speech about it at the pep rally tonight.

VERONICA. Ucch, count me out.

DUKE. Don't pop a tampon, Veronica. It was your boyfriend's idea.

*(***DEAD CHANDLER** *enters.)*

DEAD CHANDLER. Ooh, the plot thickens.

*(***VERONICA** *flinches, tries to ignore* **DEAD CHANDLER**.*)*

VERONICA. J.D.?

DUKE. He made up the signature sheet and everything.

DEAD CHANDLER. Did you hurt your finger, Veronica?

*(***DUKE** *offers the clipboard to* **VERONICA**.*)*

'Cause I notice you still haven't dialed the cops.

(VERONICA hesitates, perhaps stung by the intimation, but continues.)

VERONICA. Listen, I don't know what J.D.'s up to, but if you know what's good for you, you'll throw that clipboard away.

DUKE. Not a chance. This is very important work we're doing. I mean, now Martha Dumptruck. Where does it end?

[MUSIC NO. 17 "YO, GIRL/MEANT TO BE YOURS"]

VERONICA. What about Martha?

DUKE. They haven't announced it yet, but I hear last night she did a belly flop off the Mill Creek Bridge, holding a suicide note.

VERONICA. Oh my God.

DEAD CHANDLER. Huh. I wonder what was upsetting her.

VERONICA. …Is she alive?

DUKE. Just some broken bones. Yet another geek trying to imitate the popular people and failing miserably.

(DUKE and MCNAMARA freeze. DEAD CHANDLER, DEAD RAM, and DEAD KURT circle VERONICA.)

DEAD TEENS. *(Breathy and ominous.)*
YO, GIRL. KEEP IT TOGETHER.
I KNEW YOU WOULD COME FAR.
NOW YOU'RE TRULY A HEATHER.
SMELL HOW GANGSTA YOU ARE.

VERONICA. *(Mostly to herself.)* Martha, I'm so sorry.

DEAD TEENS & OFFSTAGE VOICES.
YO, GIRL. FEEL A BIT PUNCHY?

DEAD TEENS & OFFSTAGE VOICES.
WHAT'S THAT BRIMSTONEY SMELL?
NOW YOU'VE EARNED THAT RED SCRUNCHIE.
COME JOIN HEATHER IN HELL.

(VERONICA is now home. She runs smack into MOM and DAD, who have been waiting for her.)

DAD. Where have you been?

MOM. We've been worried sick. Your friend J.D. stopped by. He told us everything.

VERONICA. ...Everything?

DAD. Your depression. Your thoughts of suicide.

MOM. He even showed us your copy of *Moby Dick.*

(**VERONICA** *takes the book, handling it like a poisonous snake.*)

VERONICA. This is not my handwriting.

MOM. I've been on the phone all morning.

DEAD KURT. He's one step ahead of everybody.

MOM. There's a doctor in Cleveland.

DEAD RAM. Your parents, the police.

MOM. We'd like you to talk with him.

DEAD CHANDLER. He's thought of everything, Veronica.

VERONICA. What kind of doctor?

DAD. Psychiatric.

MOM. *(A warning.)* Leonard.

DAD. What?

DEAD TEENS & OFFSTAGE VOICES.
    GUESS WHO'S RIGHT DOWN THE BLOCK?

VERONICA. You're sending me to a shrink?

DEAD TEENS & OFFSTAGE VOICES.
    GUESS WHO'S CLIMBING THE STAIRS?

MOM. There's no shame in getting some help.

DEAD TEENS & OFFSTAGE VOICES.
    GUESS WHO'S PICKING YOUR LOCK?

VERONICA. I am not the problem!

DEAD TEENS & OFFSTAGE VOICES.
    TIME'S UP. GO SAY YOUR PRAYERS.

DAD. She took that well.

(*Lights change.* **VERONICA** *runs to her bedroom in a panic. Looks out the window. He's coming for her! Panicked, she hides in her closet.*)

DEAD TEENS & OFFSTAGE VOICES.
>VERONICA'S RUNNING ON, RUNNING ON FUMES NOW.
VERONICA'S TOTALLY FRIED.
VERONICA'S GOTTA BE TRIPPIN' ON 'SHROOMS NOW,
THINKIN' THAT SHE CAN HIDE.
VERONICA'S DONE FOR, THERE'S NO DOUBT NOW,
NOTIFY NEXT OF KIN.
VERONICA'S TRYING TO KEEP HIM OUT NOW.
TOO LATE –

>*(Whispered.)* HE GOT IN.

>(**J.D.** *climbs in the bedroom window, amped and darkly upbeat.*)

J.D. KNOCK KNOCK! Sorry to come in through the window. Dreadful etiquette, I know.

VERONICA. *(Offstage.)* Get out of my house!

>(**J.D.** *tries to open the closet door. It's locked.*)

J.D. Hiding in the closet? C'mon. Unlock the door.

VERONICA. *(Offstage.)* I'll scream and my parents will call the police.

J.D. All is forgiven, baby! Come out and get dressed! You're my date to the pep rally tonight!

VERONICA. *(Offstage.)* What? Why?

J.D. Our classmates *thought* they were signing a petition! You gotta come out here and see what they really signed.

>YOU CHUCKED ME OUT LIKE I WAS TRASH,
FOR THAT YOU SHOULD BE DEAD.
BUT! BUT! BUT!
THEN IT HIT ME LIKE A FLASH:
WHAT IF HIGH SCHOOL WENT AWAY INSTEAD?

>THOSE ASSHOLES ARE THE KEY!
THEY'RE KEEPING YOU AWAY FROM ME.
THEY MADE YOU BLIND,
MESSED UP YOUR MIND,
BUT I CAN SET YOU FREE!

>YOU LEFT ME AND I FELL APART,

J.D.

I PUNCHED THE WALL AND CRIED.
BAM! BAM! BAM!
THEN I FOUND YOU'D CHANGED MY HEART
AND SET LOOSE ALL THIS TRUTHFUL SHIT INSIDE!
AND SO I BUILT A BOMB.
TONIGHT OUR SCHOOL IS VIETNAM.
LET'S GUARANTEE
THEY NEVER SEE
THEIR SENIOR PROM!

I WAS MEANT TO BE YOURS!
WE WERE MEANT TO BE ONE!
DON'T GIVE UP ON ME NOW!
FINISH WHAT WE'VE BEGUN!
I WAS MEANT TO BE YOURS!

SO WHEN THE HIGH SCHOOL GYM GOES BOOM
WITH EV'RYONE INSIDE –
PCHW! PCHW! PCHW!

(Lights up to reveal a ghostly chorus of **DEAD STUDENTS**
wearing 3D glasses.)

IN THE RUBBLE OF THEIR TOMB
WE'LL PLANT THIS NOTE EXPLAINING WHY THEY DIED:

*(He rips off the top of the petition, and reads what was
concealed.)*

J.D. & DEAD STUDENTS.

"WE, THE STUDENTS OF WESTERBERG HIGH WILL DIE.
OUR BURNT BODIES MAY FIN'LLY GET THROUGH TO YOU.
YOUR SOCIETY CHURNS OUT SLAVES AND BLANKS.
NO THANKS.
SIGNED, THE STUDENTS OF WESTERBERG HIGH…
GOODBYE."

J.D.

WE'LL WATCH THE SMOKE POUR OUT THE DOORS.
BRING MARSHMALLOWS, WE'LL MAKE S'MORES.
WE CAN SMILE AND CUDDLE
WHILE THE FIRE ROARS!

DEAD STUDENTS.

    AH...

J.D.

I WAS	**DEAD STUDENTS.**
MEANT TO BE YOURS!	MEANT TO BE YOURS!
WE WERE	AH!
MEANT TO BE ONE!	MEANT TO BE ONE!
I CAN'T	AH!
MAKE IT ALONE!	MAKE IT ALONE!
FINISH WHAT WE'VE	FINISH WHAT WE'VE
BEGUN!	BEGUN!
YOU WERE MEANT TO BE	YOU WERE MEANT TO BE
MINE!	MINE!
I AM ALL THAT YOU NEED!	I AM ALL THAT YOU NEED!
YOU CARVED OPEN MY	YOU CARVED OPEN MY
HEART!	HEART!
CAN'T JUST LEAVE ME TO	CAN'T JUST LEAVE ME TO
BLEED!	BLEED!

    (**J.D.** *draws his gun.*)

VERONICA!	VERONICA!
OPEN THE, OPEN THE	
DOOR PLEASE.	
VERONICA, OPEN THE	VERONICA, OPEN THE
DOOR.	DOOR.
VERONICA!	VERONICA!
CAN WE NOT FIGHT	
ANYMORE PLEASE.	
CAN WE NOT FIGHT	CAN WE NOT FIGHT
ANYMORE.	ANYMORE.
VERONICA,	VERONICA...
SURE, YOU'RE SCARED, I'VE	
BEEN THERE.	
I CAN SET YOU FREE!	I CAN SET YOU FREE!
VERONICA,	VERONICA...
DON'T MAKE ME COME IN	
THERE.	
I'M GONNA COUNT TO	I'M GONNA COUNT TO
THREE!	THREE!

J.D.	DEAD STUDENTS.
ONE!	ONE!
TWO!	TWO!
FUCK IT!	FUCK IT!
	AH! AH! AH!

(J.D. kicks open the closet door. Scary lighting – VERONICA dangles from an improvised bedsheet noose. Dead. J.D. falls to his knees.)

(The DEAD STUDENTS exit, dispelled by J.D.'s anguish.)

J.D. Oh... God... No... Veronica...

J.D.	DEAD STUDENTS.
PLEASE... DON'T...	OO...
LEAVE ME ALONE...	
YOU... WERE...	OO...
ALL I COULD TRUST...	
I CAN'T DO THIS ALONE...	OO...
STILL, I WILL IF I MUST!	STILL, I WILL IF I MUST!

(Song ends. We hear Veronica's MOM approaching.)

MOM. *(Offstage.)* Veronica! I made you a snack. Veronica?

(J.D. hurries out the window.)

(Veronica's MOM walks in with a plate of chips and pâté. She sees VERONICA hanging and screams.)

VERONICA. Mom, Mom. It's okay!

(She reaches behind herself, releases the noose, and lands neatly on the floor. Her MOM keeps screaming.)

Mom! Stop! I'm fine. Look! See? Just a joke.

MOM. It's not funny!

VERONICA. I love you, Mom.

(Veronica's DAD enters.)

DAD. What's with all the screaming?

[MUSIC NO. 18 "DEAD GIRL WALKING (REPRISE)"]

*(**VERONICA** takes advantage of the distraction, grabs a croquet mallet, and exits.)*

MOM. It was Veronica. I found her in –

*(Notices **VERONICA** is missing.)* Veronica? Where'd she go? Veronica!

*(Lights change. **VERONICA**'s out of the house, heading for school.)*

*(**DEAD CHANDLER, DEAD RAM,** and **DEAD KURT** flank* **VERONICA,** *an invisible posse.)*

VERONICA.

I WANTED SOMEONE STRONG
WHO COULD PROTECT ME.
I LET HIS ANGER FESTER
AND INFECT ME.
HIS SOLUTION IS A LIE;
NO ONE HERE DESERVES TO
    DIE,

EXCEPT FOR ME AND THE MONSTER I CREATED!	**DEAD TEENS & OFFSTAGE VOICES.** AH, HAH! HAH! HAH!
YEAH… YEAH! HEADS UP, J.D.!	
I'M A DEAD GIRL WALKING! CAN'T HIDE FROM ME!	HEY YO WESTERBERG!
I'M A DEAD GIRL WALKING! AND THERE'S YOUR FINAL BELL;	HEY YO WESTERBERG! OH,

*(The school bell rings, signalling the beginning of the pep rally. **MCNAMARA,** other **CHEERLEADERS, STUDENTS,** and **FACULTY** enter.)*

IT'S ONE MORE DANCE AND THEN FAREWELL,	AH!
CHEEK-TO-CHEEK IN HELL WITH A DEAD GIRL… WALKING!	AH, AH AH!

STUDENTS & CHEERLEADERS.

WHOA...OA!

MCNAMARA.

Go Rottweilers!

STUDENTS & CHEERLEADERS.

WHOA...OA!

MCNAMARA.

HERE WE GO, HERE WE GO NOW!

(VERONICA approaches MS. FLEMING.)

MS. FLEMING. Veronica! Jason Dean told us you'd just committed suicide.

VERONICA. Yeah well, he's wrong about a lot of things.

MS. FLEMING. *(Vaguely disappointed.)* I threw together a lovely tribute. Especially given the short notice.

VERONICA. Ms. Fleming, what's under the gym?

MS. FLEMING. The boiler room.

VERONICA. That's it!

MS. FLEMING. Veronica, what's going on?

(VERONICA raises her croquet mallet, twirling it defiantly and stalking offstage.)

VERONICA.

GOT NO TIME TO TALK,
I'M A DEAD GIRL
WALKING!

STUDENTS & CHEERLEADERS.

HEY, YO WESTERBERG!

STUDENTS & CHEERLEADERS.

HEY, YO WESTERBERG!
TELL ME WHAT'S THAT SOUND?
HERE COMES WESTERBERG,
COMIN' TO PUT YOU IN THE GROUND!
GO GO WESTERBERG,

GIVE A GREAT BIG YELL!
WESTERBERG WILL KNOCK YOU OUT
AND SEND YOU STRAIGHT TO HELL!

(Lights change...)

Scene Seven

(The boiler room. A scary vision of hell. Machinery, steam, and creepy lighting.)

(In the middle of it all is **J.D.**, *putting the finishing touches on a time bomb.)*

*(***VERONICA*** enters, croquet mallet in hand.)*

VERONICA. A Norwegian in the boiler room. Just like your dad.

*(***J.D.*** whirls around, momentarily shocked to see her.)*

J.D. Huh. And here I thought you'd lost your taste for faking suicides.

VERONICA. Step away from the bomb.

*(***J.D.*** engages the timer on his bomb.)*

J.D. This little thing? I'd hardly call it a bomb. This is to trigger the packs of thermals upstairs in the gym. Now *those* are bombs.

(He pulls a gun on **VERONICA**. *She stands her ground.)*

People are going to look at the ashes of Westerberg and say there's a school that self-destructed not because society didn't care, but because that school *was* society. You know the only place Heathers and Marthas can truly get along is in Heaven!

*(***VERONICA*** lowers her mallet.)*

VERONICA.
I WISH YOUR MOM HAD BEEN A LITTLE STRONGER.

J.D. Don't talk about my mom.

VERONICA.
I WISH SHE'D STAYED AROUND A LITTLE LONGER.

J.D. Stop.

VERONICA.
I WISH YOUR DAD WERE GOOD;
I WISH GROWN-UPS UNDERSTOOD;
I WISH WE'D MET BEFORE

VERONICA.

THEY CONVINCED YOU LIFE IS WAR.

I WISH YOU'D COME WITH ME...

J.D.

I WISH I HAD MORE TNT!

(WHAM! **VERONICA** *whacks* **J.D.***'s gun hand with the croquet mallet.)*

J.D.   **STUDENTS & CHEERLEADERS.**

Aah!   AH...!

*(***J.D.*** and* **VERONICA** *scramble for the gun, struggling to get control of it.)*

STUDENTS & CHEERLEADERS.

HEY, YO WESTERBERG!

TELL ME WHAT'S THAT SOUND?

HERE COMES WESTERBERG,

COMIN' TO PUT YOU IN THE GROUND!

GO GO WESTERBERG,

GIVE A GREAT BIG YELL!

WESTERBERG WILL KNOCK YOU OUT AND

SEND YOU STRAIGHT TO –

(BANG! They lock eyes. Someone just got shot. We see red spreading across **J.D.***'s shirt. He collapses to the ground.)*

J.D. Was it good for you? Kinda sucked for me.

[MUSIC NO. 18A "WE'RE ALL WORTH SAVING"]

*(***VERONICA** *is torn between the inert form of her ex-boyfriend and the ticking bomb. Frantic, she looks for an off-switch, then turns to* **J.D.***, shaking him desperately.)*

VERONICA. It's over, J.D. Which wire do I pull? Which wire? J.D.!

(Too late. **J.D.** *has passed out. Or died. We can't tell.)*

*(***VERONICA** *crosses to the bomb and growls with frustration. She has no idea how to deactivate it.)*

(Upstairs at the pep rally, the stomping and clapping resumes, intercutting with dialogue. VERONICA *yells to upstairs.)*

Everybody get out! There's a bomb! You've got to evacuate!

(Nobody can hear her. The stomping and clapping continue.)

Hello! I don't know how much time we've got! Can anybody hear me?

(More stomping and clapping. VERONICA *struggles to pull the bomb from its position on the wall. Finally, she gets it loose.)*

Okay. Think. If I move the trigger bomb far enough away...

(More stomping and clapping.)

...it can't set off the thermals. Right? Right.

(She picks up the bomb and winces with pain.)

Ow!

(Her leg is injured, but she keeps going. Lights change as she moves, accompanied by more stomping and clapping.)

Dear Diary.

(More stomping and clapping.)

I still believe there's good in everyone, even the worst of us.

(More stomping and clapping.)

I believe we're all worth saving. And I guess that's a belief I'm willing to die for.

(We're outside now. The sounds of the pep rally have receded somewhat. VERONICA *stumbles, felled by her hurt leg.)*

(J.D. *appears, startling* VERONICA.*)*

J.D. You'll never make it in time. Not on that ankle.

VERONICA. How much farther?

J.D. Middle of the football field should do it. Let me take it the rest of the way.

VERONICA. No way. It's a trick.

J.D. You flatter me, but no. Look at me, I'm done for. And I'm not gonna let you die like my mom.

[MUSIC NO. 19 "FINALE (SEVENTEEN REPRISE)"]

I AM DAMAGED.
BUT YOU'RE DIFF'RENT.
YOU'RE THE ONE WE OUGHT TO SPARE.
GOD KNOWS WHY YOU WANT TO SAVE THEM,
BUT YOU BEAT ME FAIR AND SQUARE.

(He gently takes the bomb from **VERONICA**. *She lets him.)*

PLEASE STAND BACK NOW.

*(***VERONICA*** limps away from him a few feet.)*

LITTLE FURTHER.

*(***VERONICA*** limps farther, putting real distance between them.)*

DON'T KNOW WHAT THIS THING WILL DO.
HOPE YOU MISS ME.
WISH YOU'D KISS ME.
THEN YOU'D KNOW I WORSHIP YOU.

J.D.	**VERONICA.**
I'LL TRADE MY LIFE FOR YOURS.	OH MY GOD...
AND ONCE I DISAPPEAR,	
	WAIT, HOLD ON...
CLEAN UP THE MESS DOWN HERE.	NOT THIS WAY...
OUR LOVE IS GOD.	
OUR LOVE IS GOD.	
OUR LOVE IS GOD...	
OUR LOVE IS GOD...	

(**J.D.** *turns back to look at her.*)

VERONICA.

SAY HI TO GOD.

(*A loud explosion and blackout.*)

Scene Eight

(Lights up on the Westerberg corridor. **STUDENTS** *and* **FACULTY** *mill about, drawn by the noise, ad-libbing confusion.)*

PREPPY STUD. *(A little louder amidst the hubbub.)* They're saying a gas main exploded.

(VERONICA enters. Her face is blackened, hair frazzled, jacket singed. **MCNAMARA** *rushes up,* **DUKE** *a step behind.)*

MCNAMARA. Where have you been? Fleming told us you killed yourself!

DUKE. You look like hell.

VERONICA. Yeah? I just got back.

(She grabs **DUKE***.)*

DUKE. Hey!

(VERONICA removes **DUKE***'s red scrunchie and ties it over her wrist.)*

What are you doing?

(VERONICA kisses her cheek.)

VERONICA.
LISTEN UP, FOLKS.
WAR IS OVER.
BRAND-NEW SHERIFF'S COME TO TOWN.
WE ARE DONE WITH ACTING EVIL,
WE WILL LAY OUR WEAPONS DOWN.
WE'RE ALL DAMAGED,
WE'RE ALL FRIGHTENED.
WE'RE ALL FREAKS,
BUT THAT'S ALL RIGHT.
WE'LL ENDURE IT.
WE'LL SURVIVE IT.
MARTHA, ARE YOU FREE TONIGHT?

(MARTHA enters in a motorized wheelchair.)

MARTHA. What?

VERONICA. My date for the pep rally kind of blew...me off. So I was wondering if you weren't doing anything tonight, maybe we could pop some Jiffy Pop, rent some new releases? Something with a happy ending?

*(She extends a hand. **MARTHA** stares blankly, sadly.)*

MARTHA. Are there any happy endings?

VERONICA.

I CAN'T PROMISE NO MORE HEATHERS.
HIGH SCHOOL MAY NOT EVER END.
STILL, I MISS YOU.
I'D BE HONORED
IF YOU'D LET ME BE YOUR FRIEND.

MARTHA.

MY FRIEND...

*(She takes **VERONICA**'s hand.)*

VERONICA & MARTHA.

WE CAN BE SEVENTEEN.
WE CAN LEARN HOW TO CHILL.

IF NO ONE LOVES ME NOW,	**STUDENTS.**
SOMEDAY SOMEBODY WILL.	WHOA...

*(**VERONICA** extends a hand to **MCNAMARA**, who stands beside **DUKE**. **DUKE** grabs **MCNAMARA**'s arm and gives her a warning look. **MCNAMARA** isn't sure what to do.)*

PLEASE CAN WE BE SEVENTEEN?	WHOA... WHOA...
HELP US TO MAKE THINGS RIGHT	WHOA... WHOA...
WE WANT A BETTER WORLD.	WHOA...

*(**MCNAMARA** throws off **DUKE** and joins **VERONICA** and **MARTHA**.)*

VERONICA, MCNAMARA, MARTHA & GIRLS.	GUYS.
SO WHY NOT START TONIGHT?	AND YA KNOW, YA KNOW,

VERONICA, MCNAMARA, MARTHA
& GIRLS. *(Except* **DUKE.***)*   **GUYS.**
LET'S GO BE SEVENTEEN.   YA KNOW...
                                          WE CAN BE
TAKE OFF OUR SHOES   BEAUTIFUL.
AND DANCE.   YA KNOW, YA KNOW,
ACT LIKE WE'RE ALL   YA KNOW...
STILL KIDS,

(VERONICA *offers a hand of friendship to* **DUKE.** *After a beat of hesitation,* **DUKE** *takes it.)*

VERONICA, MCNAMARA, MARTHA
& GIRLS.
'CAUSE THIS COULD BE   'CAUSE THIS COULD BE
OUR FINAL   OUR FINAL,
CHANCE.   AND YA KNOW, YA
                                              KNOW
ALWAYS BE SEVENTEEN.   YA KNOW...
                                          WE CAN BE BEAUTIFUL.
CELEBRATE, YOU AND I.   YA KNOW, YA KNOW,
MAYBE WE WON'T GROW OLD...   YA KNOW...

ALL.
AND MAYBE THEN WE'LL NEVER DIE!
WE'LL MAKE IT BEAUTIFUL! WE'LL MAKE IT BEAUTIFUL!

VERONICA, MCNAMARA, MARTHA,
   GIRLS & DUKE.   **GUYS.**
BEAUTIFUL! BEAUTIFUL!   BEAUTIFUL! AH... AH...
BEAUTIFUL! BEAUTIFUL!   AH

ALL.
BEAUTIFUL! BEAUTIFUL! BEAUTIFUL! BEAUTIFUL!
BEAUTIFUL!

(Curtain.)

[MUSIC NO. 20 "BOWS"]

ONE! TWO! THREE! FOUR!

GIRLS.   **GUYS.**
NA! NA NA NA NA, NA.   NA, NA, NA, NA, NA.
NA! NA NA NA NA, NA.   NA NA, NA, NA, NA NA.
NA! NA NA NA NA, NA, NA.   NA, NA, NA, NA, NA, NA.

NA NA NA, NA, NA, NA, NA. NA NA NA, NA, NA, NA, NA.
NA! NA NA NA NA, NA NA NA NA, NA, NA, NA, NA.
NA! NA NA NA NA, NA. NA NA, NA, NA, NA NA.
NA! NA NA NA NA, NA, NA. NA, NA, NA, NA, NA, NA.
NA NA NA, NA, NA, NA, NA, NA NA NA, NA, NA, NA, NA,
NA! NA!

ALL.

WE'LL MAKE IT BEAUTIFUL. WE'LL MAKE IT BEAUTIFUL.

GIRLS. **GUYS.**

BEAUTIFUL! BEAUTIFUL! BEAUTIFUL! AH... AH... AH,
BEAUTIFUL! BEAUTIFUL!
BEAUTIFUL! BEAUTIFUL!

ALL.

BEAUTIFUL! BEAUTIFUL! BEAUTIFUL! BEAUTIFUL!

The End

"A Modest Proposal, or,
You Want Me To Adapt What?"
Laurence O'Keefe – May 7, 2015

2006: So I'm at the California Canteen, a ramshackle restaurant clinging to Ventura Boulevard right where the Valley (suburban, complacent) jams up against Hollywood (sexy, violent). Which side am I on, I wonder.

I'm there to meet my old friends Kevin Murphy and Andy Fickman, who want to convince me to help them adapt *Heathers* into a Broadway musical. This is of course a terrible idea, unless it's not.

1989: The movie *Heathers* comes out. Winona Ryder plays Veronica, a brilliant teenage misfit plucked from nerdy isolation and elevated to the ranks of the Heathers, Westerberg High School's three hottest and cruelest girls. But Veronica learns the Heathers are selfish monsters and quits to play Bonnie and Clyde with J.D. (Christian Slater), a darkly magnetic high school outlaw, who offers a cure for selfish monsters: bullets and bombs. Veronica, trapped between violence and powerlessness, must find a third solution. *Heathers* was frickin' hilarious. And it scared the crap out of everyone.

Because *Heathers* blew a whistle on our entire culture. Reagan's Morning in America had become a hungover afternoon migraine, still shilling candy-flavored lies about America the infallible. Our TVs were full of Oliver North lecturing us on how patriotism requires you to covertly sell arms to Iran and use the proceeds to finance fascist Nicaraguan rebels. Our movie theaters were stuffed to bursting with Rambos, Rockys, and almost-but-not-quite-truthful adolescent epics like John Hughes' *The Breakfast Club, Sixteen Candles,* and *Pretty in Pink.*

Those teen flicks were funny and occasionally honest about the lives of teenagers. But at heart they were candy too: utopian fantasies of Rich Boy Loves Poor Girl and Bad Boy Wins Prom Queen. We shrugged and consumed them like a Slurpee at 7-Eleven: delicious, but never mistaking it for actual nutrition.

So when a friend dragged teenaged me to see "this movie *Heathers,* about the meanest school on Earth," we had no reason to think this movie would be any less of a fantasy.

Until five minutes in when our jaws hit the floor and stayed there for two hours. It felt like a documentary about the inside of our own heads. No other movie had ever portrayed how we high school kids actually treated each other. How we sneered and cursed and lied and prayed. And how we all craved justice and safety, and how every one of us had fantasized about hurting those who hurt us.

It was cathartic. It helped me realize I wasn't alone; helped me deal with my own adolescent bewilderment and resentment and hope; and taught me to think hard about how to treat people and myself better.

So naturally *Heathers* flopped in movie theaters. But then went on to form the bedrock of our entire culture ever since. Without *Heathers* there's no *Clueless*, no *Legally Blonde*, no *Grosse Pointe Blank*, and of course, no *Mean Girls*. *Heathers'* DNA is unmistakable in *Veronica Mars*, *Freaks and Geeks*, *Beverly Hills 90210*, *My So-Called Life*, *Dawson's Creek*, and on and on and on.

2006: Problem is, I tell Kevin and Andy, *Heathers* also spawned smug stories celebrating shiny, rich, defiantly mean girls: *Gossip Girl*, *Pretty Little Liars*, *My Super Sweet 16*, *Laguna Beach*. Without *Heathers*, there would be no TV shows for Paris Hilton, Kim Kardashian, and Real Housewives everywhere.

Heathers looked so gorgeous, and the actors so deliciously hot and effortlessly cool, that many audiences forgot the film's satire and anti-violence stance, and instead worshipped the candy-coating, treating the fashions, hairdos, and mansions as a consumer Bible. So wouldn't a *Heathers* musical fall into that trap? Wouldn't a musical adaptation soften the wrong edges and wind up glorifying glamorous cruelty?

"Guys," I said, "We have a hard choice: stay true to the dark heart of the movie and risk alienating Broadway audiences, or soften the edges for theatergoers' tastes and dilute the honesty that made the film iconic in the first place.

"Broadway audiences aren't the same as film audiences; they usually expect higher levels of hope and optimism and much, much lower levels of teenage sex, teenage murder, and (worst of all!) teenage swearing. In a Broadway house a light PG can feel like an R.

"And part of what makes the film so delicious is its moral poker face. It has so much fun showing misfit teens wreaking murderous revenge that it's hard to tell whether the filmmakers deplore violence or endorse it. Not until the very last few minutes, when Veronica finally decides, 'No, blowing up my school will not save it.' She stops J.D.'s murderous plan, then confronts Heather Duke, the new alpha dog. She rips the red scrunchie of power from Duke's hair and ties it around her own, declaring, 'There's a new sheriff in town,' then turns to poor wheelchair-bound loser Martha Dumptruck, inviting her over to watch videos. Only then do we understand that the screenwriter, Dan Waters, prefers forgiveness over violence. Till then the movie can feel a bit like a dispatch from a free-fire zone in one of those ancient trouble spots where no UN-brokered ceasefire ever holds.

"And even if we find a way to make theatre audiences okay with the racier stuff, in the end will they even want to hear the movie's message that change is rare and painful? That when you depose one Heather you risk becoming a Heather yourself? Broadway audiences prefer their morals black-and-white and their endings uplifting-and-victorious: *Hairspray*, *The Lion King*, *Legally Blonde*. They don't love having their assumptions challenged.

"I mean, *Sweeney Todd* is a masterpiece and it's been produced on Broadway three times, but none of those three times was a box office hit. And this movie is often even more nihilistic than *Sweeney...*"

They replied: "Sure, the movie is. But Larry, your own musical *Bat Boy* ends with a stage littered with bodies, which is played for laughs, and audiences still found it moving. *Avenue Q* and *Urinetown* are hilarious and yet stay honest and deal with real darkness. We think a musical *Heathers* can be less flippant about violence than the film and still hit hard. It's the story of a teenage girl trapped in an abusive pressure-cooker environment, who longs for a better world, but makes destructive mistakes until she learns to separate justice from revenge. That can sing."

They had me. I took the leap of faith. Wasn't hard, actually. Kevin and Andy are geniuses and have hearts full of hilarity and warmth. They created one of history's funniest musicals, *Reefer Madness*. They've made lots of great television and movies. And you can't get more dedicated champions for a project than our three originating producers: Amy Powers, J. Todd Harris, and Andy Cohen. I'm glad I joined them. It's been the best professional experience of my career.

But mostly I knew they had me when Kevin Murphy showed me his first draft of a lyric for a song called "My Dead Gay Son."

"The Writing Process, or,
Does He Have To Pull Out A Magnum In The
Lunchroom?"
Kevin Murphy – May 8, 2015

"Although it is expertly done, can you draw sweet water from a foul well?"

– Brooks Atkinson, reviewing the original 1940 production of *Pal Joey*

One of the useful things about being a working television writer is that studios pay you enough money to subsidize either a medium-sized cocaine habit or a black box Equity Waiver theater stage musical every ten years or so. Andy Fickman and I had gone down the latter path producing *Reefer Madness* in the late nineties, so by 2006 we were about due for the next production, *Heathers*, which we figured would be easier on our nasal passages than the alternative.

Securing the underlying rights took the better part of a year. Securing the services of the obscenely talented Larry O'Keefe took another few months. I have to confess, I was spooked when Larry initially failed to display the same enthusiasm for adapting *Heathers* that I felt. Maybe he was right. That Brooks Atkinson quote (above) nagged at me. After all, the source material is famous and beloved for the dissociative, nihilistic manner in which the characters deny human emotion. "Chaos is what killed the dinosaurs, darling!" "I say we grow up, be adults and die." "Whether or not to kill yourself is one of the most important decisions a teenager can make." Cool, ironic detachment is certain death in a medium in which characters feel emotions so deeply and intensely that they can only be expressed in song. What if the world of *Heathers* was too emotionally arid to be adapted into a watchable musical entertainment? I had to find out.

I decided to start with a character song for J.D., as he was the character that scared me the most. He scared me because he's a psychopath. He scared me because he brings a Magnum to school and straps a big-ass bomb to his chest. He scared me because he's a serial killer and proud of it. But mostly, he scared me because I didn't understand him. In the original film, J.D. is unknowable, enigmatic, and distant. His backstory is hinted at in the screenplay, we're given tantalizing glimpses into his twisted co-dependency with Big Bud Dean, but aside from the pivotal story of his mother's death, the movie audience is largely left to fill in the blanks for themselves, ably assisted by the megawatt movie-star charisma of Christian Slater. Unfortunately, our stage musical wouldn't have the benefit of a lingering close-up on his face. Movie stars have mystique – they engage the audience by withholding. No matter how fantastic a young actor we found to play J.D., he would always be on a stage, at least twenty feet away from the nearest audience member. It all had to be there in the music and the text.

I reasoned that if I could successfully get inside J.D.'s head and create an engaging character-defining soliloquy for him, then the rest of the show would be a piece of cake. (It wasn't, but these are the lies writers tell themselves early in the creative process.) I started by asking myself what J.D. wants. He wants to be left alone. He wants to stay disconnected and detached. He recoils from any sort of human connection. Trouble was, these are all negative, unattractive ideas, and the plot dictated that J.D. had to seduce Veronica with this song. I knew that by the end of Act One Veronica (and the audience) would see this character for what he truly is: an unrepentant multiple-murderer. If we didn't make Veronica (and the audience) fall in love with him early on, the entire undertaking was doomed. But how do you make misanthropic isolation sexy?

Stumped, I watched the movie again. An idea in it resonated with me in a new way – J.D. was an itinerant kid, dragged from town to town by his father's dodgy, probably illegal work. J.D. had no friends. No roots. The only consistent part of his life was the 7-Eleven convenience store (changed to Snappy Snack Shack for the finished film, but 7-Eleven in Dan's original screenplay). No matter what city, every single 7-Eleven was exactly the same with the exact same microwave burritos and Slurpees. J.D.'s character statement song would be a romantic tribute to the reassuring symmetry of 7-Eleven shops everywhere. The Slurpee would be J.D.'s drug of choice, and he would revel in the brief, painful oblivion of the signature ice cream headache you get from slurping it too quickly.

Everything tumbled together after that and the lyrics only improved once Larry came aboard (finally!) and started contributing new ideas. J.D. became an articulate, insightful huckster who is instantly attracted to our wickedly smart, self-loathing heroine. He instinctively understands that a big-hearted girl like Veronica will be a sucker for a hard-luck story delivered with wit, charm, and a frosty carbonated beverage. And once Larry set the lyric to music, I realized something important. I really, really liked this J.D. kid. I liked his fierce intelligence, his kill-or-be-killed survivor skill set, and I felt genuine empathy for how shitty his life had been since his mom died. And I especially liked him because he appreciated the specialness of our leading lady. No matter what bad choices this guy makes, his love for Veronica remains unwavering and pure. I suppose there's a sort of Travis Bickle rule that applies here: We forgive a psycho killer who is doing it all for love.

That was going to be the key to adapting *Heathers*. We had to find ways to like everybody. Even though pretty much every character in the story is cruel, selfish, angry, and/or deluded. We had to find ways to transform negative into positive.

How hard could that be?

Another song lyric I worked on during those early pre-Larry months was

"My Dead Gay Son." In the movie, it's a brief mordant joke – homophobic jock asshole dad expresses love for his gay son for no other reason than because he's dead. A gay son with a pulse would presumably have been thrown out of the house or worse. It's a very funny comic moment indelibly linked to the very ugly reality of homophobia. I wasn't thinking about any of that, though. This was a case of me falling in love with a song title, pure and simple. I was deeply enamored with the idea of a big fat hand-clappin' gospel number at the jocks' funeral.

I remember showing a first draft of the "Dead Gay Son" lyric to Larry while sitting at the Coffee Bean on 3rd & La Cienega trying to convince him to join our team. Larry appreciated that the lyric was a high-calorie confection – packed with fun jokes and rhyming, loopy metaphors and naughty double entendres – but, as he rightly pointed out, the number lacked heart. It was clever, but an essentially shallow enterprise. The townspeople singing were clueless sheep, the dads were both unlikeable hypocrites, and the fantasy version of the jocks that appeared in the number were camp cartoons.

As we dug deeper into the lyric, Larry hit on a most amazing notion – what if the two dads shared a secret *Brokeback Mountain* love? A love that has haunted and shamed them ever since that confusing and eventful fishing trip back in 1983. And it is only through the (false) bravery of their two sons that one dad is empowered to proclaim his love to his soulmate in the middle of a crowded church. To my way of thinking, that gave us high-stakes emotion well worth singing about. And by the time we were done, you know what? I really liked our two dads.

And so it goes. As we wrote, re-wrote, and refined, Larry and I wrestled hard to mine the hidden positives in these characters, absent or only hinted at in the film. To make sure our heroine Veronica was a character in whom the audience would want to invest, we added an opening number "prequel" that explains how terrifying life at Westerberg High can be and shows how Veronica resourcefully uses brains, charm, and talent to J. Pierrepont Finch her way into the coolest clique in the school. Ms. Fleming is a buffoonish media whore in the film, and we kept her that way in the musical, but we also worked to tease out some laudable qualities in the character – she genuinely means well and busts her ass to make the school a better place.

Veronica's parents are recognizable as the blandly cheerful automatons from the original film, but we worked to add some real moments to their brief time onstage and had Mom deliver a prescient warning to her daughter to not dump long-time best friend Martha for the Heathers. We greatly expanded the character of Martha from the film, blending her with Betty Finn to create a clueless-but-lovable dreamer of a bestie. The jocks both remain horrible jackasses in the musical, but we included a new scene with their dads to help us understand how they became that way – pointing out how environment can stunt emotional growth and empathy in young people.

Heather McNamara is weak and vapid, so we wrote the song "Lifeboat" to help audiences connect to the character, suggesting that beautiful cheerleaders are every bit as scared and insecure as the rest of us. By the end of Act One, Heather Duke is revealed to be a nasty piece of work, but we tried to depict her as so relentlessly and consistently abused by Heather Chandler that the audience at least understands and respects the abject terror that fuels her ruthless ambition.

Our take on *Heathers* suggests that these characters are not necessarily bad people. They are the human product that results when you take several hundred young people at the most hormonally ravaged, physically awkward, and emotionally insecure period of their lives and dump them into a giant social terrarium with minimal supervision. The chaos and cruelty that ensues is unsurprising.

The message of the original movie is, according to screenwriter Dan Waters, "The heart dies when you're twelve." If our musical has any message at all, it might be, "The heart hits the floor and goes into a terrified defensive crouch when you're twelve. The great challenge of high school is to help it up and back into your chest where it belongs."

Heathers The Musical may not be anyone's idea of sweet water, but if you suck it down hard enough, you get one hell of a brain freeze.

This article was originally published on *Breaking Character* as part of the *Heathers The Musical* series. *Breaking Character* is Concord Theatricals' online theatre magazine for theatre makers around the nation, providing the latest industry news, engaging content, and best resources. For more information, visit www.breakingcharacter.com.

Heathers Writers Laurence O'Keefe and Kevin Murphy Break Down the Musical's Full Album Track by Track

Laurence O'Keefe & Kevin Murphy – March 22, 2018

What is the new song replacing "Blue" in the score? Plus, learn the motivation behind each melody and more.

When *Heathers The Musical* debuted Off-Broadway in 2014, the rock musical gained a cult following just like that of its cinematic predecessor. Written by Laurence O'Keefe and Kevin Murphy, the musical adapted Daniel Waters' film about Veronica Sawyer's quest to fit in with the hottest high school clique, the Heathers (Heather Chandler, Heather McNamara, and Heather Duke), while falling for an unhinged vigilante classmate.

The show was first presented as a concert at Joe's Pub at the Public in downtown Manhattan in 2010, starring Annaleigh Ashford as Veronica and Jeremy Jordan as Jason Dean (aka J.D.). In 2013, the show played Los Angeles' Hudson Backstage Theatre before a run at New World Stages Off-Broadway.

But what earned the show's place in the upper echelon of niche hits is its smart writing in libretto and music, and its references to the movie while carving an identity of its own.

"One of the tricks we learned to use in the show is using positive language to convey ugly ideas and depict cruel behavior," the writing team tells *Playbill*. "We tried our best to have our characters express positivity even when they're doing terrible things. This outlook is more conducive to fun songs than one dwelling on misery and negativity, and it sets a tone that affords the audience permission to laugh even while exploring serious issues like bullying, teen suicide, and violence in schools."

Here, Murphy and O'Keefe take a deep look into the plot points, movie references, and musical scoring in this track-by-track breakdown of the *Heathers* cast album.

ACT ONE

"Beautiful"

Call us crazy, but when we first saw *Heathers* the movie, we didn't just see a cruel nightmare high school dystopia. We both saw a girl trying to make her world better and more just. In the movie, Veronica has a great diary entry:

"Heather told me she teaches people real life. She said, real life sucks losers dry. You want to fuck with the eagles, you have to learn to fly. I said, so, you teach people how to spread their wings and fly? She said, yes. I said, you're beautiful."

Very early in our writing process, we made a list of ideas from the film that might lend themselves to songs. The word "beautiful" was at the top. We loved that it's a word that can be used sarcastically, as Dan does in his screenplay, but it's also an aspirational word. We love the original film, so it was important to us to honor the plot, but one question Dan Waters chose not to answer in his screenplay was how, when, and where Veronica got invited to join the three Heathers. "Beautiful" came out of a desire to answer that question and explain the social pressures that drove a kind, bright, and sensitive young woman like Veronica to start changing herself to try to belong to the alien world of the popular kids.

In composing the music, a fun rhythmic idea kept asserting itself: a missing beat. Meaning, the intro vamp that weaves throughout the song is only fifteen beats long, instead of a symmetrical sixteen (so every fourth measure is a 3/4 bar instead of a 4/4). That means new verses and important events show up a beat earlier than expected, crashing the party too soon. It helps keep audiences off-balance, showing that these characters are often hurried and harried, and that this world is out of joint.

"Candy Store"

This replaced an earlier song called "Human Connection," which was well-crafted, solid, and professional, but which never fully landed. That original song showed Heather Chandler using twisty Orwellian logic to smarmily justify her cruelty to Martha. ("WE MAKE HER SMILE, WE DRY HER TEARS...") We realized this approach weakened Chandler's character. As undisputed dictator of the school, Chandler would have no reason to lie. She fears nobody and nothing, so she readily admits to Veronica that she enjoys hurting people because she can. Adhering to our rule of keeping the language and ideas aspirational, we dug deeper and found a song that makes Heather's cruelty feel fierce and joyful.

We knew we needed a distinctive rhythm and feel, and this is one of the only pieces in the show in 6/8 time. We were hoping for something menacing and industrial, maybe with a feel like Depeche Mode or Alice In Chains or even the fierce stomping triplet-feel pop songs of the Katy Perry/Britney era. Then we got the pit band in, and with the live horns it sounded totally different from what we'd envisioned: a more retro sound that felt a bit like Ann-Margret and Amy Winehouse were throwing a party with En Vogue. A happy accident and fun to dance to too.

"Fight For Me"

This is a sneaky, manipulative number, and yet a heartfelt song. In "Fight For Me," Veronica gets a guilty erotic charge from watching myst hot new kid J.D. kicking the crap out of two bullies. [Director' Fickman's brilliant slow-motion staging was laugh-out-loud fun consistently stopped the show. By the end of the number, the audience is cheering and applauding a violent act of retaliation. This sets the necessary tone for the rest of the story early on, helping the audience feel okay laughing at some pretty harsh and cruel stuff, while building evidence to make our later argument that harsh and cruel behavior is no laughing matter.

Musically, this song is one of our favorite bits of 1980s timbre and color. While throughout the score we tried to avoid resorting to clichéd eighties harmonies and melodies, we sure enjoyed boning up on the keyboard textures and guitar pedals used in many eighties ballads. Shout out to chorused guitars and Roland electric piano.

"Freeze Your Brain"

This was one of the first songs we wrote and an important litmus for us. We were writing a story in which a smart young woman falls in love with a psychopath in J.D. If we couldn't make the psychopath sexy, sympathetic, and worthy of our heroine's time and interest, we had no show. The central metaphor was inspired by one of the poems from *Flowers of Evil*. The Baudelaire version (translated from French) is:

"You have to be always drunk. That's all there is to it – it's the only way. So as not to feel the horrible burden of time that breaks your back and bends you to the earth You have to be continually drunk."

J.D.'s numbing agent of choice is a Slurpee.

(By the way, sometimes people ask why we changed the name of the convenience store. In the film, this scene happens in the "Snappy Snack Shack" and in the musical it takes place in a 7-Eleven. The answer is that we're honoring the source material; it's 7-Eleven in Dan's original screenplay. They couldn't get permission to set the scene in a 7-Eleven and were forced to change. For similar reasons, the high school in the musical version is spelled "Westerberg" instead of "Westerburg." The studio executives thought "Westerberg" would look too Jewish on the signage and asked that the spelling be changed. Since the school was originally named for Paul Westerberg, the lead singer of Winona Ryder's favorite band, we decided to reinstate the correct spelling.)

Anyway, "Freeze Your Brain" was designed to feel like the inside of J.D.'s brain: seemingly clear and forthright, but leading the listener gradually into stranger and stranger places. At any given moment the chords make sense, but they keep mutating into new chords, patterns, and keys. As J.D.'s rage builds, the accompaniment climbs higher and the keys keep changing with it. Each chorus ends with three chords (call them "VI flat – IV minor – I minor") that show up in many other songs in this show, including "Dead Girl Walking" and "Seventeen." We don't know if it qualifies as a leitmotiv, but you might call it a musical idea, and it tends to crop up around moments in which a lead character refuses to submit to fate. That wasn't a conscious compositional plan, but we like to pretend it was.

"Big Fun"

This replaced an earlier party song called "Beer and Booze," which had a rowdy, shouted Beastie Boys feel:

"BOOZE AND BEER! BEER AND BOOZE! A PARTY'S NOT A PARTY TILL YOU PUKE ON YOUR SHOES! RUNNING IN YOUR UNDERPANTS LIKE TOM CRUISE! CHUG! CHUG! CHUG! BRING DAT BOOZE!"

That feel was juxtaposed with a bouncy patter song for Veronica wandering through the party, disgusted by the gross drunken antics of her classmates, dreaming of escaping high school and finally arriving at the promised land of college. But this didn't satisfy. We felt it was more powerful to show Veronica having a blast at the party. That way, she makes a real sacrifice when she dares to oppose Heather Chandler. Once again applying our aspirational language maxim, we decided the party should be "Big Fun," which is an iconic phrase from the original film. Plus, it's a fun eighties dance song with lots of rubbery bass, chorus guitar, and gated snare drum. Music to trash your parents' house to. Dude.

"Dead Girl Walking"

At this point in the movie, Veronica has just been excommunicated by Chandler. Veronica returns home and descends into self-pity, writing angrily in her diary. J.D. surprises her by climbing in her window. But for the musical adaptation we wanted Veronica to sing here, processing the enormity of what she's just sacrificed and the danger she's put herself in. In the musical, Veronica drives the plot forward more consistently than in the movie, and we didn't want to take our foot off the accelerator, so we realized it was stronger to have Veronica be the one initiating things. So Veronica throws all caution to the wind and "celebrates" her final moments by climbing into J.D.'s room and bluntly seducing him.

This song is a pivotal transition for J.D. Later, in "Our Love Is God," J.D. sings:

"I WAS ALONE. I WAS A FROZEN LAKE. BUT THEN YOU MELTED ME AWAKE – SEE, NOW I'M CRYING TOO."

This is the moment where that begins. If Veronica had left well enough alone and stayed out of J.D.'s life, he would have probably kept his murderous rage frozen and dormant. In teaching J.D. to love, she inadvertently awakens a sleeping monster. Compositionally, this song is a melting pot; there must be a dozen musical genres thrown in, genres ranging from AC/DC to Pink Floyd to Stevie Wonder to Sondheim to Kurt Weill. We knew this one had to be both funky and metal, both a lamentation and a celebration, both a howl of despair and a party war cry. It might be our favorite song.

"The Me Inside Of Me"

Despite the epic scope of this song, it was relatively easy to write because by this point in our writing process, we'd written several other songs and fully understood our positive language rule. The text of Heather Chandler's fake suicide note was noble and aspirational and helped us show our very human tendency to glom onto someone else's tragedy and make it all about ourselves. There is a nice soupy, mawkish quality to this fake anthem, evoking memories of those self-indulgent charity singles like "We Are The World" and "Do They Know It's Christmas?" that were so popular in the eighties. While this is one of our most traditional-Broadway songs, we kept trying to change up the tropes. Verses full of Sondheim and Weill darkness followed by uplifting pop choruses that could be sung by Lionel Richie at Live Aid. And this is one where we gave in to our constant urge to change keys in the middle of a verse. It's just so fun! But it does wreak havoc on vocal arrangements. We're lucky our singers didn't murder us. Especially our altos.

"Blue"

By the time you read this, the song "Blue" will have been retired. We're now in the process of replacing the song for all future amateur and professional productions. It has been replaced by the far superior song "You're Welcome," which we wrote for the *Heathers High School Edition*. Some fans miss "Blue," so we might as well say a word about it.

Although it was fun to write and it's fun to perform, "Blue" has always been polarizing. Some thought "Blue" was wonderful and all in good fun. Others were offended, feeling we were treating date rape as a laughing matter. It went onto our list of things we knew we needed to alter or replace. As happens in musicals, you reach a point at which you've run out of rehearsal time and are forced to lock the show as-is. That's what happened with "Blue." For us, the main issue with "Blue" is that it was lazy. It's a variation on that old musical theatre trope, the "list song," and it lacked any real or human insight into the idea of date rape and the culture of teenage male entitlement that allows it to exist. Additionally, the fact that the number often plays successfully makes it dangerous. It plays into the lie that sexual harassment or assault can be trivialized as "locker room talk" or "boyish antics." Unlike "Blue," "You're Welcome" doesn't shy away from showing that Veronica is in real danger from these two drunk football assholes. In "Blue," Veronica says about three words total. In "You're Welcome," she gets to articulate her fear and her dilemma, and then she gets to solve her problem and score a victory over her tormentors. We've tried to do a better job with "You're Welcome," and we hope audiences agree as *Heathers* moves into the next phase of its life.

"Our Love Is God"

At this point, Veronica has been publicly humiliated, and J.D. has been beaten up by Kurt and Ram. Our lovers are at their absolute low point.

They comfort each other by imagining the destruction of this cruel and insane world and starting over. We took the title for the song from one of the many iconic lines in the movie. When J.D. says, "Our love is God. Let's go get a slushie," Christian Slater delivers it in a rakish, off-the-cuff manner. But that first sentence really resonated with us. "Our love is God." Wow. It's an incredibly narcissistic thing to say, but that's how we remember feeling about relationships in high school. On the other hand, it's also the kind of thing a serial killer would say to justify his actions. Throughout the first half of the song, this seems like a romantic notion, a "you and me against the world" empowerment fantasy. We were kind of imagining a sort of alternate-universe version of *West Side Story*'s "Somewhere" where Tony and Maria fantasize about an asteroid obliterating the cruel world that keeps them apart. The twist comes when J.D. reveals that he's not being metaphorical.

After killing Kurt and Ram, J.D. reprises this refrain:

"I WORSHIP YOU. I'D TRADE MY LIFE FOR YOURS. WE'LL MAKE THEM DISAPPEAR; WE'LL PLANT OUR GARDEN HERE... OUR LOVE IS GOD."

It's nearly the exact same words and music he sings earlier in the song, but having just committed two murders, he no longer sounds like a dreamy rebel. Veronica and the audience now realize he is a dangerous psychopath.

Compositionally, this was a fun musical puzzle. We needed a melodic and harmonic vocabulary that could serve in the early, gentle verses as a sensitive emo ballad, but then turn terrifying once J.D. has shot Ram and Kurt, as the unseen scary choir swells behind the murder scene. We shared a J.D. grin when we hit on a bassline that rises slowly for the first four bars, then climbs down ominously for the next four: sort of a climb toward heaven followed by a slide into hell.

ACT TWO

"My Dead Gay Son"

The original, iconic movie joke – while hilariously depicting Ram's homophobic, conservative dad changing his heart because he's been fooled into thinking his son was gay and his death a suicide – wasn't quite enough to sustain a full song. We needed more surprise, more plot, and more heart. So we added a plot twist: Ram's dad sings not just to declare his change of heart, but to chastise and educate Kurt's dad, who can't let go of his own homophobia and shame. Then we added an even bigger plot twist, which we don't want to spoil here.

Rather than write these dads as goofy and out of touch, we tried to explore the real emotions of fathers processing horror and grief, struggling to overcome their own fear and shame and replace it with love and kindness.

"Seventeen"

The first draft of this was titled "Damage." We wanted Veronica here to take a stand not found in the original film. She gives J.D. an ultimatum: Stop murdering people and try to be a human being, or you lose me forever. What would be Veronica's best argument to wake J.D.'s humanity up and arrest his slide into rage and madness? You have to offer hope of something better. We recalled some of our personal high school histories, when as teenagers we'd had to intervene to try to save people, although we weren't qualified and the job should never have fallen to us. We had thrown up our hands in defeat, thinking, "Can't we just be seventeen?"

The music here seems to be a favorite for a lot of people. We think it could be partly due to that weird unexpected V-minor chord under "can't we be seven-TEEN." We also like that even this ballad has that missing-beat phrase (thirty-one beats instead of thirty-two in the chorus).

Plus, we've discovered there seems to be no limit to how slow "Seventeen" can be sung. It seems the slower you sing it, the stronger the emotional impact. It might someday break "My Heart Will Go On" for the slowest pop single in history. Of course, first we have to get someone to put it out as a single. Anybody know Beyoncé?

"Shine A Light"

The last song we wrote before opening in New York, about a month before previews. (Sorry, Michelle.) We'd tried earlier versions of this school assembly scene, when Mrs. Fleming tries to stop the "suicide epidemic" by engineering a big public kumbaya spectacle to encourage kids to let down their guards. Having sat through similar well-meaning, excruciatingly awkward assemblies in high school, we wanted to capture that weird energy you get watching an authority figure whose heartfelt performance can't quite conceal some distracting personal issues. Strangely, until this song we'd never tried having Fleming herself sing.

The music has a utopian sixties feel – we are all children of "Free To Be You And Me," the Jackson Five, and *Hair* – but we also wanted it to feel like the music of high school educational videos. It was fun to imagine some 1980s board meeting at Scholastic Productions where some creative exec says, "We gotta start using this thing the kids are all going nuts for, it's called 'rap'..."

"Lifeboat"

This is where Heather McNamara falls for Fleming's kumbaya bait and reveals her fears to the whole assembly. Researchers in adolescent psychology have described being in high school as being like trapped in a very small lifeboat. Crammed in a tiny, unstable space with far too many of your peers, you're trailing behind a huge ocean liner containing all your teachers and parents. The grown-ups are tethered to you by a thin rope, but too far away to appreciate the danger you're in. That metaphor felt appropriate for Heather Mac, and it's been gratifying to see the audience's understanding of Mac change instantly. And we like that it's the simplest song in the show. Just one key change!

"Shine A Light (Reprise)"

Heather Duke gleefully humiliates Mac for her public confession and drives her out of the assembly to try to overdose on pills. The audience always gets a fun jolt of dark energy watching Duke pervert Fleming's utopian song and weaponize it, getting inside Mac's head and driving her to despair. A fun, nightmarish moment, but we always felt bad for the actors playing Duke, because this is one of Duke's few short solo moments in the show...for now. That may change very soon. You heard it here first.

"Kindergarten Boyfriend"

One of the authors was actually engaged to be married, at age five, to a kindergarten classmate. Sadly, by first grade her family moved away. Years later we get to turn painful memories into money. Thanks, Becky, wherever you are.

Kevin brought in an early lyric draft to Larry and asked if it could be a song. ("Sure, the scan and imagery are great...but hang on, where are the rhymes?" asked Larry. "Exactly," said Kevin.) We had both grown up with Sondheim's dictum that rhymes connote education or sophistication. So we realized that at this point in the show, with Martha's kindergarten boyfriend dead and gone, she is so beyond caring about earthly things that she wouldn't even bother to rhyme. Musically, we enjoyed holding back all orchestrational forces as long as possible, using only piano, waiting until the final bridge to unleash a glorious fanfare as Martha soars away into her fantasy world with the love of her life.

"Yo Girl & Meant To Be Yours"

These two songs are really one sequence. This was a fun adaptation and a slight departure from the film, calling both for psychological and logistical changes. For the musical adaptation, we felt we needed to dig deep into J.D.'s psyche, to find the core of grief, loneliness, wounded pride, rage, and desperate love that could drive a teenage boy to kill dozens in an insane attempt to remove the obstacles (i.e. people) he thinks are preventing his beloved from loving him. Even though in the movie J.D. thinks Veronica is dead at this point, to amplify the urgency we had J.D. start the song thinking Veronica's alive, still trying to win her over to his awesome romantic murder plan. J.D. sings his monstrous manifesto to a Veronica who has locked herself in her closet. Only at the end of the song does J.D. kick down the closet door, discovering Veronica (apparently) dead.

And of course this song is the hardest music in the show. (Sorry, J.D.s. And music directors.) Lots of dropped beats, meter change-ups, key changes, the whole kitchen sink, in keeping with J.D.'s frantic mental state. But again the positivity rule helped us – J.D. sees his murderous plan as a solution to win back love and make the world a better place.

And we like that every few months someone tells us, "Omigod, I only just noticed that the melody of the dead teens singing, 'Yo, girl, keep it together' is exactly the same melody as J.D.'s 'I was meant to be yours.'" Thanks for noticing!

"Dead Girl Walking (Reprise)"

Our Positivity Doctrine helped us a lot here. Here is where we really tried to write a *Heathers* for our current era. The original movie did a great job blowing the whistle on the lies and self-deceptions of the Reagan era. But once you've blown the whistle, what then? It wasn't enough for our stage version to just replicate those criticisms. We needed to take a further step, and clarify that we, and *Heathers The Musical*, abhor violence, and we have to keep looking for ways to help angry people before they lash out in anger; and that we have to change the ways our schools and communities are run and prioritized. And so in these angry and often brutal times, we try to remember that Veronica believed that J.D. was redeemable all the way to the end. She reached out to him instead of pushing him away. It seems a good way to live.

"I Am Damaged/Seventeen (Reprise)"

Another pair of songs that's really one song, and another departure from the movie scene.

We were also excited to realize that in a happy accident we could smoothly segue a reprise of "Seventeen"…

"'CAUSE YOU BEAT ME FAIR AND SQUARE. PLEASE STAND BACK NOW…LITTLE FURTHER. DON'T KNOW WHAT THIS THING WILL DO. HOPE YOU'LL MISS ME. WISH YOU'D KISS ME –"

…into a reprise of "Our Love Is God":

"– THEN YOU'D KNOW I WORSHIP YOU. I'LL TRADE MY LIFE FOR YOURS. AND ONCE I DISAPPEAR, CLEAN UP THE MESS DOWN HERE…"

We were surprised (and relieved) to realize that no new song did a better job of ending this show on a high note than a simple reprise of "Seventeen." It seemed to encapsulate Veronica's journey from fear (thinking there's this huge monolithic monster called "SCHOOL" out to get her) – to acceptance (realizing that SCHOOL is made up of individuals just as scared, human, and redeemable as she is). That's the real love story in *Heathers*. Veronica and J.D. are the doomed love story; the real love story is Veronica and her flawed yet redeemable classmates.

This song contained another moment that wasn't finished until we were nearly in previews. When Martha re-enters in her wheelchair and Veronica invites her over to eat popcorn and watch videos, we originally had Martha agree immediately, which felt rushed. So in one of our last adjustments before we opened, we gave Veronica a moment to apologize to Martha. Giving Martha time to listen to Veronica, and forgive her, made a difference. It made the song more vulnerable, and, according to our actors, it caused some really good ugly cry faces in the audience every night. So looks like we did at least one thing a bit right.

Thanks for letting us ramble! We appreciate you reading. We're honored. Our love is God. Shut up Heather, Kevin & Larry.

This article originally appeared on *Playbill.com* on March 22, 2018.